Becoming Somebody

By H. D'Agostino

Becoming Somebody

H.D'Agostino

The following story contains mature themes, profanity, and graphic sexual situations. It is intended for adult readers.

Cover design by Kari March at K23Design

Photography: Kelsey Keeton of K. Keeton Designs

Models: Cameo Hopper and Storm Bailey

Editing by Rebecca Cartee @ Editing by Rebecca

ISBN: 978-0-9907704-6-6

Table of Contents

Prologue

As the door to the jet closed, and the engines began to speed up, I sank down into one of the plush seats. My mother was staring out the window pensively as I fought the sobs trying to consume me. It was happening again. We were leaving… again.

"I can't do this anymore," I wiped at my eyes as I watched the world blur past me. The plane picked up speed, and we left Chicago heading to who knew where.

"Honey," my mom turned her head to glance at me.

"Don't!" I held my hand up to stop her as I growled.

"Sam," she sighed. "You know if I could change things, I would."

I dropped my shoulders dejectedly as I wrapped my arms around my middle, "I love him."

"I know." She reached for me as she slid from her seat and moved beside me. "I know you do."

"I'm always giving up what I want. When am I going to get something back? When?" My voice rose from an ominous growl to shrieking howl. "He loves me," I pointed at my chest as I turned to look up at her. "Me. He wants me. Why couldn't I stay? Why?"

"You know the answer to that," she soothed. "He did, too."

"Do you even know where we're going?" I sat up a little straighter and scanned the cabin for Kevin.

"Nevada," Kevin nodded as he went back to the laptop that was sitting in his lap.

"And who am I this time?" I huffed.

"Sam," he warned.

"I know, I know," I rolled my eyes as the last of my tears began to dry on my cheeks.

"Your name is Jennifer, and you're a waitress." He handed me a manila folder before going back to what he was working on. "I'm looking at apartments right now. I should have you all set by the time we land. It'll be a hotel for tonight."

"Fan-freaking-tastic," I muttered as I shifted in the seat. This was just great... another bar I'm sure, and another dead-end job to go with it.

oooooooooo

A week went by before I started my new job, and surprisingly, it wasn't as bad as I'd thought it would be. I was working in the restaurant portion of The Venice Casino. It was high-end clientele, and the men didn't seem to be as grabby. My boss, Andy, seemed nice, too. It didn't hurt that he was hot, but I knew the rules. I couldn't get involved, and to tell you truth, I didn't really want to. My life was crazy enough, and in the back of my mind, I had hopes that Dev would find me. He had promised he would, but I knew from past experience that some promises were easily broken or forgotten, especially when you were looking for someone that the government was trying to hide.

The apartment that Kevin had found was small, but it worked. It was right outside of Vegas, and my mother's was only two blocks away. I had asked about us sharing one, but my mother insisted that I was young and needed my space. I couldn't argue with that, but I didn't really see myself bringing anyone home anytime soon.

"We're pretty slow here tonight," Andy came waltzing through the tables where I was wiping them down. It was near the end of my shift, and my feet were killing me.

"Yeah, but it sure was busy earlier," I smiled as I arranged the salt and pepper shakers.

"Why don't you take off after you finish that set-up? I can have someone else finish this," he smiled at me, and I knew by the look in his eyes that he was secretly thinking about something else. "Hey, Jen?" he grinned. Here it goes… I could see it playing out in his expression. "You wanna grab a drink sometime? Or maybe a coffee after your shift?"

I closed my eyes as I thought about what I wanted to say. This was my boss. I wasn't looking to date anyone. I couldn't. I couldn't tell him who I was. I couldn't give him my heart; Dev had it. I also didn't want to make things awkward here at work. He was cute though, and the way he was standing there expectantly made something inside of me crack a little.

"I don't know, Andy," I looked away. "I've got a lot going on in my life."

"Just drinks," he smiled. "I'm not looking for marriage."

"Just drinks?" I crossed my arms over my chest. "Am I missing something here?"

"I want to get to know you better," he shrugged. "We'll see where it goes from there."

"All right, fine," I laughed. "Drinks. Give me an hour and I'll meet you back here, but I'd rather have coffee instead of alcohol. I haven't been feeling the best for the last few days."

"Everything ok?" His grin morphed into a look of concern.

"Yeah," I nodded. "I think I'm just run down. I've had a lot happen in my life recently. I'm trying to get back on track, but it's gonna take some time."

"Coffee sounds great. See you in an hour," he turned to walk away, but quickly spun to face me once again, "Hey Jen, relax," he smirked. "I don't bite."

I giggled, "Yeah, ok," as I felt my stomach roll once again. Maybe going out tonight wasn't such a good idea. Maybe I should be in bed trying to get over whatever this was wreaking havoc on my stomach. Maybe I should just stop questioning everything I do. Maybe I should just say screw it and let Andy in. I've always wanted to be somebody to someone, and Andy seemed to want me. Could he help heal my broken heart? Could he help me become someone? Only time would tell.

Chapter 1

Four Years Later...

As the sun slowly rose and began to shine through the curtains, the body beside me shifted. I snuggled deeper into the covers and burrowed into his embrace.

"Good morning," he mumbled as he placed a light kiss to the top of my head.

"Mmmm," I murmured. "It's not morning yet. I'm still tired."

"Did I wear you out last night?" he chuckled as he dipped his chin to capture my lips.

"No," I whispered.

"Jen," he teased.

"You're so full of yourself," I jabbed my finger into his side causing him to flinch away from me. It was short lived, but the pain at hearing him call me Jen was still there. I was never gonna be Sam to him. I'd always be Jen, and he'd never think differently.

"We better get up, or we're gonna have a repeat of last week," he warned.

Before I could respond, the bedroom door burst open, and a whirl of messy blonde locks came barreling into the room. "Mommy!" she squealed as she launched herself onto the bed and forced herself between us.

"Morning, baby," I smiled as I brushed my daughter's hair back out of her eyes. "Did you sleep well? No more monsters?"

"Yep," she grinned as she shoved her finger into her mouth. "Can we do something fun today? You promised that when it was nice, we'd do something fun. So can we? Please, can we?"

"Mara," I yawned as I glanced out the window and then back at her. She looked so happy, and her innocence was something to be jealous of. She didn't know my life, and it looked as if she would never have to. We'd been in Nevada since she was born and unless forced to, or the threat disappeared, I didn't plan to uproot her.

"Ask Andy," I whispered as I grinned.

"Can we, Daddy?" she clasped her hands under her chin and stuck her lips out in a pout. "Please?"

"Can you clean up your room?" He tried to look stern, but failed miserably.

"Un huh," she nodded.

"And get dressed?" he chuckled.

"Yeah, yeah," she rocked back on her heals as if she was ready to pounce.

"Then I suppose we could go to the park later," he shrugged as he rolled toward me. "What do you think, honey?"

"Sounds good to me," I smiled before looking back at Mara.

"Yippee!" she squealed as she launched herself off the bed and scampered out of our room.

"You sure you're not too tired?" Andy reached for me and tugged me into his arms. "You sure didn't want to get up earlier."

"I'm fine," I sighed as I let him wrap himself around me, "but we do need to get up."

"Fine," he groaned as he released me and sat up. He swung his legs over the edge of the bed and stood. I watched him walk toward our bathroom and grinned when he paused in the doorway. "You should take a picture; it'll last longer," he called.

"I'd rather stare, thank you," I giggled as I watched him shake his head. Andy was good looking, and he seemed to get even better looking with age. He was older than I was, but it didn't seem to bother him. Having Mara didn't bother him either. I was thankful for that in many ways. Being a single mom on the run was hard enough, but having the man in my life not accept her would have made it so much worse.

I found out about Mara shortly after moving to Nevada. Andy had been my boss, but when we started dating, I quit the restaurant gig. Now I worked as a cocktail waitress in the casino. It paid more, and I could still be close to him just not working for him. Mara and I moved into his house when she was just a baby, and we've been there ever since. It works for us, and Mara sees him as her father. He's not, but she doesn't need to know that. I couldn't have asked for a better man. He'll never know what I've been through to get here, but I guess that's good in a way.

I haven't heard from Kevin in over six months.
The trial has been slow, and they haven't
needed me to testify yet. Kevin did tell me that
I'd have to go back to Chicago whenever that
happened, but that could still be months away.
Andy thinks that Kevin's my cousin, and that
we have family in Chicago. In a way, that's
true, I guess. That's the last place Dev was,
and he's family now, whether he knows it or
not. Kevin won't tell me where he is, and he
hasn't contacted me. I don't know how he
would though. He doesn't know Jennifer; he
knows Mallory.

oooooooooo

It was a beautiful day in Vegas. The sun was
high, and even though it was hot, it wasn't
terrible. The park was only a few miles from
Andy's house, and as soon as we got there,
Mara practically launched herself out of the
car.

"Honey, wait for us!" I shouted as I watched her
bounce toward the swings.

"You're too slow!" she giggled as she
continued at top speed.

"Relax," Andy soothed. "She's fine."

I nodded in agreement, but inside I was
screaming at the top of my lungs 'no, she's
not'. No one understood my protectiveness

over her. They saw me as a hovering parent. They didn't know that every day I feared for her safety. Sure, George didn't know where I was. He hadn't sent any of his goons after me from what I could tell. No one from my past knew about her, but I kept envisioning someone grabbing her. She was the only thing I couldn't lose.

"She's such a daredevil," I sighed. "I'm worried she's gonna hurt herself."

"She's a kid; kids get hurt. She needs to be independent. You've got to let her do things for herself," Andy reached for my hand. He laced his fingers in mine and began leading me over to a park bench under a nearby tree. "You can see her just fine from here," he mumbled as he felt me resist slightly.

"Yeah, ok," I muttered just as my phone began to vibrate in my pocket. I held up my hand to signal that I needed a minute as I tugged the phone out to check the caller ID. It was Kevin, and my heart fluttered in my chest. Every time he called me, I prayed that he'd have news about Dev. I needed to know he was ok, that he'd made it out ok, and that George wasn't after him. "Hey," I answered hesitantly.

"Sam. Can you talk?" His voice was low and quiet.

"Not really," I grumbled. "I'm at the park with Andy."

"I know," Kevin's voice echoed through the line. "I'm watching you right now."

"What?" I gasped as I began frantically searching the area for the telltale sign of the Marshals. There was no van, no dark sedan, no nothing. "Where?"

"Look to your six," the line clicked off as I spun around.

There, off in the distance, was a dark figure straddling a motorcycle. His hand rose in acknowledgement and I nodded as I began walking back over to where Andy was sitting. "Can you watch her for a minute? I need to use the Ladies Room," I pointed to the out building several feet away.

"Sure," he smiled at me. "Take your time. We'll be fine."

"Thanks," I darted my eyes to where Mara was playing, and then turned and briskly headed over to Kevin, who now stood beside the back with his helmet off.

"What's going on?" I panicked. "Is everything ok? Is it Dev? Did something happen?"

"Sam," he sighed. "Breathe." He stuffed his phone in his pocket and flipped his sunglasses up on top of his head. "Let's go over here," he motioned to a spot in the shade.

"Ok, but what's going on?" I began pacing around. It wasn't like Kevin to beat around the bush. He never held back and was always brutally honest.

"It's over," his eyes looked relieved, and suddenly, the weight that this whole ordeal had put on him was blatantly obvious.

"What?" I placed my hands on top of my head and slowly dragged them down my face.

"The trial. It's over. George is in prison," his mouth turned up in a crooked smile.

"But what about me? How come no one had to talk to me?" Confused by this new information, my emotions had yet to catch up to my brain.

"We had enough taped evidence from your dad, and between the undercover work, and the new witnesses that have come forward, we didn't need you," he placed his hand on my shoulder. "It's over. You can go home now. Back to New York. You can be Sam again."

"I don't even know who that is anymore," I mumbled.

"I thought you'd be happy about this," he gripped the back of his neck.

"I'm confused. I know I'm supposed to be happy, but things are good right now. I have Mara, Andy, a home, and job... I sort of have everything I've wanted."

"But are you happy?" Kevin's head tilted to the side as he stared at me.

"I don't know what happy feels like; it's been so long. I've learned to be good at faking it," I glanced over to where Mara was still playing on the swings. "She thinks Andy's her dad. She doesn't even know *him*..." I trailed off.

"I don't know where he is right now, but I do know that he was calling Chicago 'home base' for a while. He needs to know about her, and you need to be the one to tell him," he sighed as he looked in the same direction I was. "If you're happy here, then stay, but I think you're fooling yourself."

"There's no thinking about it. I just..." I paused as I watched my daughter run into my boyfriend's arms and laugh. "How do I tell him? What do I tell him? He loves me, and he doesn't even know who I am?"

"Tell him the truth," Kevin flipped his sunglasses back down. "Tell him everything. If he loves you like you think he does, then he'll understand."

"I don't know if I can. I've been lying to him for so long. He's gonna wonder why I never told him the truth."

"You have to try," Kevin glanced over at Andy one last time before he turned and headed back to his bike. "If you're happy here, stay, but if you want to go anywhere," he waved his hand in the air, "let me know, and I'll help you."

"Anywhere?" I lifted my brows.

"Anywhere," he gave a quick jerk of his head as he swung his leg over the bike.

"Thanks," I smiled at him, "for everything."

"You're welcome," his voice softened as he slipped his helmet on and cranked the bike. "If you need anything, call me." Before I could answer, the bike lurched forward and Kevin took off.

oooooooo

"Mommy?" Mara's voice trembled slightly. "Where are we going?"

I'd told Andy about everything as soon as we'd gotten back home. It didn't go well to put it mildly. His face had paled as I watched him fight to find his footing. I was taking everything he knew about me and blowing it to bits. He'd waited until Mara went into her room to play before he'd exploded. "I can't believe you

~ 20 ~

fucking lied to me! Don't I mean anything to you? Did you not think you could trust me?" he slapped at his chest. "What about her?" he pointed at Mara's closed door.

"She's not yours." I cried as the anger that I'd repressed for years rose to the surface. "You know that!"

"She doesn't!" he bellowed. "She thinks I'm her Daddy. How are you going to explain that one?"

"I don't know yet," I muttered as I pinched the bridge of my nose. "I'll figure it out."

"Like hell you will!" He stormed over to stand toe-to-toe with me.

"Don't threaten me," I hissed. "I've been dealing with this crap since I was seven."

Andy's anger deflated as fast as it had appeared, "I'm sorry. I'm sorry you went through that. I'm sorry you felt like you couldn't tell me," he slumped down in a chair and buried his head in his hands. "Is this why you kept turning me down? You felt like you couldn't tell me who you were?"

"It's part of it," I mumbled. "Andy," I moved beside him and cupped his cheek. "I didn't know if I'd have to leave again. I didn't want to drag you into this. If I'd told you, then you'd have to come with me."

"I would have, you know? I would have given up everything." He looked up at me with sad eyes.

"I know. I think that's part of the reason I didn't tell you. This life isn't an easy one," I let my hand fall. "I've got to go back. I have to tell *him* about her."

"What?" Andy gasped.

I refused to look at him. I knew I'd see his pain. "He needs to know."

"So you've already decided this? I don't even get a say?" He shook his head.

"I told you; she's not yours. Can you honestly tell me that if things were different and she was yours, and you didn't know about her, that you'd be ok with that?" I turned to face him and the look on his face almost broke my heart.

He nodded slowly, "I love you. You know that right?"

"I know," I whispered.

"And you know I'd do anything for you… right?" He touched my shoulder as he stood.

I nodded as I stared out the window.

"I hope you find what you're looking for. But I can't help but think that you aren't coming back. You're gonna pack up and take her who knows where, and I'm never gonna see you again, am I?" he mumbled.

"I'm sorry," I let the tears fall as pain seized my chest. "I have to do this. I have to try."

"I know," he nodded as he turned and walked away. I heard his keys jingle then the door softly close as he left.

ooooooooo

"We're going on a trip." I forced myself to smile as I watched her watch me.

"Where?" Her head tipped to the side as she observed me.

"Chicago," I smiled at her. "It's where Mommy used to live."

"Why?" Mara's tiny voice squeaked.

"There's some people there that I want to visit," I ruffled her hair. "You ask a lot of questions."

"Is Daddy coming, too?" She hopped off the bed and scampered toward to the door to look into the hallway.

"No, baby," I zipped the last suitcase shut and heaved it to the floor.

"Why not?" Her little face contorted as she tried to process everything.

"He needs to stay here. This is just a trip for us," I pulled the handle up on my luggage and began heading to the front door. "Mara?" I turned to face her.

"Yeah, Mommy?" she grinned as she placed the ear of her stuffed bunny into her mouth and began chewing on it.

"I love you," I smiled at her.

"I love you, too," she giggled as she began to bounce. "Can we go on our 'venture now?"

"'Venture?" I wrinkled my forehead.

"Yeah!" she clapped excitedly. "You said that this trip could be a 'venture. I'm ready to go."

"Yes, baby... this can be our adventure," I looked one last time at the house I'd called home for the last three and half years before backing out of the driveway. I'd told Andy I'd be back, but I knew in my heart that I wouldn't. I wasn't just going Chicago to try to find Dev; I was going back to the one place that I thought could bring me true happiness.

Chapter 2

It took us two days of driving to get to Chicago, and by the time we arrived, I was completely fine with never getting in my car again. The trip had been long and somewhat boring. Mara had been a little trooper, though. For an almost four year old, she barely complained, and spent most of the trip watching movies on her tablet. The weather had been great. Sunny days and mild nights, the perfect summer weather.

When we approached the city, the lights in the distance had just begun to turn on. "Ooh!" Mara looked wide-eyed out the window. "It's so pretty, Mommy."

"You think?" I grinned at her. Watching her experience the city for the first time was mesmerizing. She'd seen Vegas, but this was different.

"Are we gonna get out soon?" She shifted in her car seat and tugged at the straps. "I'm tired of sitting."

"Yeah, baby. We are almost to the hotel. Just a few more minutes," I sighed as I took the last turn and made my way into downtown. Nothing had really changed since I'd left. People were scurrying around as the nightlife came alive. Bars were beginning to light up and taxies cruised by.

When I neared my old apartment building, waves of memories filled my head. My brain began replaying the last time I had been there. The fear I'd felt as I raced down the streets trying to get to safety. I remembered the confusion that assaulted me when Brian had beaten down my door then spilled his secrets to me. I thought about the bar, and Tori, Tiff, and Lauren. I wondered where they were, and how things were going. Lost in my thoughts, I almost drove past the hotel where I'd booked a room. It was a block down the street from The Rusty Nail, and I was hoping to be able to grab some dinner somewhere close by.

"We're here," I called as I glanced in the rear-view mirror at my daughter. She smiled and kicked her feet.

"Yeah!" she squealed and clapped her hands. Then she looked at me, and crinkled her nose. "How come Daddy didn't come with us?"

I wasn't sure how to tell her this. How was I going to explain that Andy wasn't her daddy? What if I couldn't find Dev? Should she grow up without knowing the truth? Would Dev want her if I found him?

"Mommy?" Mara cocked her head to the side. "What's wrong?"

"Nothing, sweetie. Let's get checked in. We'll get some food, and if you eat all your dinner, maybe we can go swimming," I grinned at her.

"Tonight?" she giggled. "But it'll be bedtime soon," she mused as she looked out the window. It was getting dark and that meant bedtime.

"You're right, but you can stay up a little later tonight. We're here. We're gonna celebrate our adventure," I winked at her.

"Really?" she shrieked with excitement.

I nodded as I pulled into a parking space and cut the engine. I blew out a breath and squeezed my eyes shut for a moment as I let reality take hold of me. I was back. I was gonna find him. I had no idea where to start, but I was gonna find him.

oooooooooo

The evening had been pretty uneventful and, after a nice swim in the hotel pool, Mara had passed out from exhaustion. I, however, stayed up into wee hours of the morning. I stared out the wall of windows in our room and surveyed the city. My mind had wandered in so many directions the night before that I was unsure where to start.

I yawned, watching the sky turn a light shade of gray, as the sun rose in the distance. The city lights began going off one at a time as morning approached. The one thing that I'd noticed the night before were the lights at The Rusty Nail. They hadn't come on, which I thought was odd. Tori never closed. When I was working there, we'd begged her to stop opening for lunch, and she'd never agreed to it. Now, I couldn't believe that she would close on a Friday night. Fridays were a money night.

As I rose from the chair I'd been perched in, I stretched my arms over my head, and groaned as my body protested. It'd been a long time since I'd voluntarily stayed up all night. With Mara, I'd been forced to when she was fussy or sick, but last night she'd been neither. My thoughts had kept me up. My brain wouldn't turn off, and I knew that until I found Dev, it probably never would.

"Mommy?" Mara rubbed her eyes as she rolled over in the bed.

"Good Morning, sweetie," I smiled at her as I made my way over and sat on the edge of the bed beside her. I gently pushed some of her blonde curls back off her forehead with my fingertips as I studied her appearance. Her lips curled up on one side as she stared me. She shared that smile with her father. Even as an infant, I could see him in her: the chocolate eyes and crooked smile. She was the spitting image of him.

"What's wrong?" She pushed herself up and studied me.

"Nothing, honey. We have a busy day, but how about we get dressed and go get some breakfast? Maybe," I tapped my chin and pretended to think for a minute. "Chocolate chip pancakes?"

"Yippee," Mara clapped as she scurried out of the bed and into the bathroom. "Can we do something fun today?" her muffled voice called out.

"We'll see," I sighed and shook my head at her question. This was an everyday inquiry, and not having Andy here to say yes was going to leave me in a bind. As much as I wanted to have a million fun days, I really needed to do some research and investigative work.

Once we'd gotten dressed, Mara and I headed down the elevator to the lobby. We were going to walk today. It was nice out, and I missed this part of city life. In Nevada, I lived in the suburbs and needed a car to go practically anywhere. Here, I could walk and show Mara places that I used to know.

When we'd gotten out onto the sidewalk, I turned left and began heading to toward The Rusty Nail. I'd missed my friends and was hoping that maybe Tori was inside doing the books. Maybe, if I explained what had happened, and why I'd left, I could get her to give me a job. I still hadn't figured out what I was going to do about money. I had savings, and the money my dad had left me when he died, but I couldn't live off that forever. I wanted to secure a future for Mara, and I was secretly hoping that maybe one of Dev's contacts would wander in one night.

Lost in my thoughts, I almost walked right by the place. I stopped abruptly and stared. A 'Closed' sign hung in the window. I cupped my hands around my eyes and leaned closer to the glass. When I saw the inside, I gasped.

Chairs were up on tables, and the room was cloaked in darkness. Dust covered the bar, and all the liquor bottles were gone.

"Mommy?" Mara tugged at my shirt trying to get my attention. "What is this place?"

"Mommy used to work here," I mumbled absentmindedly.

"Place's closed," a voice behind me called.

"Huh?" I spun to see a woman climbing out of a car parked on the street.

She shrugged as she clicked the lock button on her key fob, "Think it's been that way for about a year. Don't know what happened, but the owner just up and left it. Bank's been trying to sell the place for a while, but nobody's been interested."

"Thanks," I murmured, turning to look in the window once more.

"Mommy, I'm hungry," Mara whined. "Can we eat now?"

"Yeah, baby." I grabbed her hand and began walking away. "We'll go eat now." As we strolled down the street, heading for the diner on the corner, I couldn't help but let my mind drift back to the bar. It was as if everything that had once meant something to me was disappearing. Dev was nowhere to be seen, and now the one place that I'd practically lived in was gone, too. Chicago wasn't looking as promising as I'd once thought it would. I was beginning to question my decision to come back when Mara, of all people, had a revelation.

"Mommy?" she looked up at me as I opened the door to the diner. "Why don't you open it back up?"

I crinkled my eyes in confusion as she peered up at me. She looked at me as if it was the simplest thing in the world. "Open what?"

"That place. You said you worked there," she pointed from where we'd come.

"Oh, I don't know honey. That would be a lot of money. Mommy would have to work a lot, too," I sighed as the idea began to take root in my head.

"I could help you," she smiled sweetly.

"I know you could. You're a great helper. I think I'd have to get Grandma to help, too. I don't know if she'd want to come back here," I mumbled.

"Please, Mommy," Mara rocked up on the balls of her feet, and wrapped her arms around my legs. "It'd be a 'venture," she giggled.

"How about we eat breakfast, and then we'll talk about it?" I ruffled her hair.

"Ok," she jerked her head in a quick bob as she looked around. "I'm hungry."

"Well, then," I began leading her to a table, "let's eat."

Once seated, I stared out the window as Mara began coloring on the child's menu. The idea of owning The Rusty Nail seemed like an impossible dream. There were so many things that I'd need to do to make that happen. I'd need help, that was a given. I'd need someone to look after Mara. I'd need money, and I wasn't even sure how to go about owning a business. What had happened, and where was Tori? Things must have been pretty bad if she ended up closing the place. That woman had said the bank owned it. That meant Tori had let it go into foreclosure.

The more I thought about it, the more I wanted to do it, but I knew it wasn't going to be easy. "Mommy?" Mara reached across the table and tapped my arm. When I looked up, our waitress was standing at the end of the table waiting for my order.

"Oh," I was jolted from my thoughts; I hadn't heard her approach. "I'm sorry."

"It's ok," she smiled at me. "What can I get ya?"

"Chocolate chip pancakes with two plates, a coffee, and a chocolate milk with a lid," I smiled as Mara bounced in her seat.

"You got it," the waitress grinned as she spun on her heel and rushed back into the kitchen.

"Mommy?" Mara paused in her coloring, "I like this 'venture."

"Me too, baby, me too," I mumbled as I went back to staring out the window and letting my mind wander. I had to make this happen. It was a sign. I know it was sign.

Chapter 3

After finishing our breakfast, Mara and I went to the local library a few blocks away. They had a children's section with a large castle she could sit in while she looked at books, and it was within eyesight of the reference section. I wanted to be as prepared as I could be when I called Kevin. He'd promised me he would help, and I was going to take him up on his offer.

I think I'd spent most of the day searching through the pile of books I'd collected, and honestly, I probably would have stayed longer if Mara hadn't come to ask me for lunch. It was hard having her with me. Back in Nevada, she spent her days in pre-school. I'd pick her up on my way home from work each day, and we'd talk about whatever she had learned. Now that we were here, I knew I needed to work out our living situation. I needed a place to stay for the long term, and I needed a job. My list of things to do seemed to be growing by the hour, and I was suddenly feeling overwhelmed.

"Mara," I called as I stacked the books on the table where I was sitting. "Let's go. We've been here all day. Mommy needs to make a few calls, and you can watch some TV back in the room."

"Ok," she yawned when she appeared at my side.

"Seems the time difference is catching up with you," I smiled at her.

She shrugged, "When's Daddy coming? Doesn't he miss me?"

"Mara," I sighed as I squatted down in front of her. "Daddy's not coming on this trip. We've talked about this," I cupped her cheek when she tried to turn away from me.

"Why? Doesn't he miss me?" She stuck her lip out and it slowly began to quiver.

"Of course, he loves you, but there are other people that love you, too, and they used to live here. I want you to meet them." I watched her, hoping she'd accept my answer and not push for more. I wasn't sure if I'd ever find Dev, and I didn't want to tell her about him until I knew they could meet. It would be easier for her to understand when she was older if I never found him.

"We're not going back home... are we?" Tears welled in her eyes as a crease formed along her brow.

"No, baby, we're not, but I called Grandma earlier, and she's coming here," I tried to stand, but Mara held fast to me keeping me in place.

"I want to go home," she released me, and crossed her arms over her chest. "I want to go see Daddy."

I closed my eyes and paused for a minute before looking back into her sad brown eyes, "This is home now. I promise that you're gonna like it."

"No!" she stomped her foot and cried.

"Mara," I soothed. "Let's go." I pointed to the door, lifted my purse onto my shoulder, and began tugging her along with me. I knew we were making a scene, and even though I didn't need to hide anymore, I still didn't want to bring unwanted attention. Mara didn't normally act like this, and I wasn't sure if it was a phase, if she was just tired, or if she was acting out because I'd uprooted her. Was leaving Andy behind really the best decision for me? I was beginning to think I should have asked him to come with me.

oooooooooo

After a nap that afternoon, things seemed to settle back down, and as Mara watched cartoons, I called Kevin. I'd told him what I wanted to do and asked for his help. I even had a list. I wanted to get an apartment somewhere close to the bar, and I needed to find a pre-school for Mara. Since my mom had agreed to come out to help, I needed a place for her to stay, and most of all I needed Kevin to hook me up with a realtor. I wanted to buy the bar, not just rent the space. I had no experience running a business, and I needed Kevin to sign for me. He'd laughed like he didn't think I was serious, but he finally agreed.

Now, exactly eight weeks later, things were finally in place. I'd moved into a small two-bedroom place not far from the bar. What it lacked in size, it made up for in location. So much had changed over the last four years that I almost didn't recognize the building, but when Kevin met me in the parking lot, I knew exactly why he'd picked it.

"I thought it was only fitting," he smirked.

"How'd you know?" I glanced around at the large warehouse turned apartment building.

"He's my nephew," Kevin shrugged. "I might not know where he is, but I do know that he used to live here."

"What makes you think I want to deal with those memories every day?" I muttered.

"We can look somewhere else," he glanced around. "I just thought…"

"No, I like it here, and Mara will, too." I smiled and strode toward the building.

It took me a little over a week to settle in, but I now owned a condo instead of renting an apartment. Mara seemed happy. I could tell she missed Nevada and Andy, but her new school was only a five-minute drive away. She'd made a couple of friends and was happy to have my mother around. Everything seemed to be happening just like I'd wanted, except finding Dev.

"Where are you," I mumbled at the sky every night. He'd said he'd find me. I'd done everything I could to make it easy for him. I'd changed my name back to Sam. I was living in the last place we'd been together. I'd even bought a condo in his building. I'd bought the bar and was only a week away from opening it. Last week, I'd even gone by the police station and asked if they could give me any information on his whereabouts. When they'd found out that I wasn't even family, they'd laughed at me. Family members weren't allowed to know the whereabouts of undercovers, so why would an ex-girlfriend?

oooooooooo

The day before the bar was set to open, I was sitting at a table going over inventory. The staff I'd hired was busy setting everything up and organizing the liquor. It felt weird being back. I still didn't spend much time in the office. No one questioned it, but the corner had become my makeshift office. It felt strange being in the back; that had always been Tori's spot, and even though I was now the boss, I still thought of it as hers.

"Hey, Sam?" Chris, a bartender I'd just hired the day before, called from where he was bent over behind the bar "We don't have any bottled Buds back here. Did the truck come in yet?"

"No," I called back as I slumped against my seat. I thought things were going well, but it seemed that little issues kept coming up. "Can you ask Meredith to call the supplier?" I'd hired Meredith as an assistant manager right after I'd started renovating. She'd been a lifesaver through all of it. She played the role that used to be mine.

"Sure thing," he replied as he rounded the corner toward the back.

"Holy shit!" said a shrill voice that caused my head to jerk upwards. "It is you!" I blinked a few times as the owner of the voice came scurrying toward me.

"Tiff?" I gasped.

She nodded and slid into the booth across from me. "Where the hell have you been?"

"Uh," I stuttered. "How did you?" I glanced at the door and then back at her.

"It's not locked," she rolled her eyes. "When I walked by here last week, I saw that somebody had bought the place. I wanted to see if I could get a job, but the guy that was here said that the owner had gone home for the night."

I slowly nodded as I listened to her excited voice. She smiled at me as she reached across the table and grabbed my hands, "So you work here now? Since when? Where have you been, Mallory? You just didn't show up one day, and now you're back?"

"Tiff?" I shook her hands as I tried to get her stop and look at me.

"What is it?" Her forehead creased in confusion.

"How much time do you have? I'll tell you everything, but it's gonna take time."

"I've got all day," she grinned.

"Ok," I blew out a breath. I pointed at her, "Listen and no interrupting."

"Promise," she giggled. "Did that hot piece kidnap you or something?"

"Tiff," I warned.

"Sorry," she sat back and placed her elbows on the table in front of her.

I spent the next half hour spilling my guts. I told her everything. How I'd been running my entire life, about Dev, about Kevin, how I'd had to leave because George was going to find me. I told her about stopping in to get my check and running for my life back to my apartment. I told her about moving to Nevada, and right when I was getting ready to tell her about Mara... in she comes.

"Mooommmmmmyyyy!" Mara came barreling through the door with my mother right behind her.

"Hey," I smiled as I met my mother's gaze. I'm sure I looked confused. Normally, when my mom picked Mara up, they went back to the condo and waited for me to come home.

"She wanted to see you. We weren't sure when you'd get home tonight. I know you're opening tomorrow," my mom came over and stood near me. "I can take her home if you want."

"No, give her a few minutes. There's pizza on the bar if you guys want a slice. We ordered earlier for the employees that stayed to finish setting up. I think it's still warm."

"Great," Mom's shoulders slumped. "She wears me out, sometimes."

I laughed before looking back at Tiff, "This is Mara... my daughter."

Tiff stared for a moment as she watched Mara bounce on the seat near me before getting up and heading to the bar with grandma. Tiff's eyes darted back and forth, before she dared to voice the question that I could see in her eyes, "Is she?"

"Yeah," I mumbled. I hadn't gotten to finish my story from earlier, "I need to find him, and I'm back to do that, among other things."

"Wow!" Tiff gasped. "I can't believe it. All that time and I thought..." she trailed off.

"Everyone thought," I assured her. "It was my job to keep it all a secret. I couldn't tell anybody."

"So what does this mean now?" She looked around. My mom had made her way over to the pizza and was helping Mara up onto a stool.

"I'm going open up this place tomorrow and try, with everything I have, to give her a normal life," I nodded in my daughter's direction. "I hope that one day, he'll come back here. It's his last known place of residence. I honestly don't know other than that," I swallowed to hold back the tears. My chest hurt from all the pain I'd been fighting to hide the last several weeks. I knew that if I let myself feel any of it, I'd never be able to stop. "So, you still want a job?"

"Yeah," Tiff grinned. "Is the owner around?" She swung her gaze around wildly.

"Tiff," I sighed. "I'm the owner," I pointed at my chest.

"But, I thought?" her mouth dropped open.

"I bought this place," I laughed, "and if you want a job, it's yours."

"Seriously?" She shook her head as if she was trying to make sure that she understood what I was saying.

"Yeah. You can start tomorrow. I need more bartenders. I know you know your stuff. What'dya say?"

"I'm in," she held her hand out across the table so I could shake. "I'm so in."

"We open at 4. You need to be here by 3:30," I grinned.

"No lunch shift?" she smirked. She knew the battle we'd fought with Tori over lunch hours.

"I looked at the old financials. Tori left a bunch of paperwork in her office. Staying open at lunch put this place in the red. If we do well, then maybe later, but right now we're an evening only bar with a happy hour," I handed her some papers. "Fill this out, and bring it in tomorrow. You can wear your old shirts if you still have them. I'm not changing a thing other than the hours of operation. Things used to be good here," I answered her confused expression. "I want them to be good again, and I think you're just the person I need to do it."

"Wow!" she gasped. "Thanks."

"No problem. Just don't let me down." I nodded in Mara's direction, "The success of this place is what's determining her future. I put everything I have into re-opening this place."

"I hear ya," she glanced toward the door. "I'll see you tomorrow and thanks."

"You're welcome," I smiled as I watched her step through the door, and out onto the sidewalk. "Hey Mara," I slid the papers that were in front of me over to the side, and waited for her to turn around.

She spun on the barstool and looked at me all wide-eyed, "Yeah?"

"Let's go home," I smiled.

"Really?" she giggled as my mom's mouth dropped open.

"There's nothing I can't do here in the morning, and I won't be home tomorrow night before you go to bed." I shrugged.

"Yippee!" she squealed as she jumped down and ran into my open arms. "It's ok," I murmured to my mom as she came over. "I've got this. You're gonna have her a lot over the next few days. I'll take her the rest of the night."

"Are you sure?" Mom placed her hand on my shoulder. "I really don't mind."

"You've been a lifesaver, Mom, but I need time with my baby." I smiled at her as I released Mara from my embrace. I stood and wrapped my mom in a hug. "Really, it's fine. I'll see you tomorrow."

"All right, see you tomorrow," she mused as she released me and turned to leave.

"Hey, Chris," I called.

"Yeah Boss," he looked up from where he was stacking things.

"You can go home. We're closing for the night. We can finish this before we open tomorrow."

"Thanks," he waved, grabbed his jacket, and then breezed by me. When he reached the door, he grabbed the handle and paused, "Hey, Boss?"

"What is it?" I rubbed at my eyes as I gabbed some of the papers off the table I'd been sitting at.

"You waiting on a ride or anything?" He glanced back at Mara and me.

"No… why?" I mumbled absentmindedly.

"No reason," he called as stepped out the door. "See you tomorrow."

After turning off the lights to the front of the place, I dug my keys out of my purse, locked the front door, and grabbed Mara's hand. We began walking down the sidewalk to where I'd parked my car. Out of the corner of my eye, I saw movement. At first, I didn't think anything of it. It was only seven-thirty at night. People were still out and about, but the feeling that crept over me began sending out a sense of foreboding. Something wasn't right.

I quickly picked up the pace, almost dragging Mara, as I took the last few steps to reach my car. I quickly unlocked it and rushed Mara in. After buckling her in her car seat, I rounded the front end, and opened my door. I paused to look back in the direction we'd come, that's when I saw it. Hidden in the shadows away from the streetlights, a dark figured straddled a motorcycle across the street from the bar. It was just dark enough to hide him, but the chill that sank into my bones brought back all the old feelings. He was wearing a helmet, and when I paused to stare, he quickly cranked his bike and took off.

It took a minute for me to react, but as I climbed in and locked my doors, panic began to set in. Who was that, and why were they watching me? Did George have reach from the inside? He was in prison, and according to Kevin, I was safe. I knew I needed to call him and report this, but at the moment, my fight or flight instinct was kicking in, and it was telling me to run. I had a child now, and I needed to protect her. I needed to get home where it was safe, and then I'd figure out my next move. I knew one thing for sure: I was done hiding. I was going to figure this out and fight it. I just needed to make sure Mara was safe first.

Chapter 4

After hastily tucking Mara in, I crept out into the living area of our condo and began pacing. I knew what I should do, but the possibility of losing the freedom I'd just recently gained scared me. I couldn't go back to the life I'd just fought so hard to escape. I chewed on my nails nervously as I wandered into the kitchen. After pouring myself a glass of wine, I grabbed my phone and began alternating between convincing myself to call Kevin and telling myself I was being stupid. Fear for Mara's safety won out, and I begrudgingly called the only person I could think of that could give me answers.

"Hello," Kevin's voice was cheerful, not at all like it usually is.

"I need your help," I blurted out as I sank down on the couch.

"Sam? What's wrong?" The lightness in his tone quickly disappeared, and the stern all business tone I was used to appeared.

"I don't know exactly," I murmured. I closed my eyes and blew out a breath as I went into the tale of my day. Kevin listened intently on the other end of the line as I rambled before I finally reached the point of taking a breath.

"Sam! Calm down! I know you're worried, but this doesn't seem right. You're safe, I promise," he soothed.

"How can you be sure? I feel so exposed now," I panicked.

"I know it's going to be hard for you to trust people," he grumbled as he cursed under his breath, "This is why I didn't want you coming back here."

"But why would he be staring at me? Are you sure?" My voice raised an octave as I stood and stormed over to the window.

"Sam," he attempted to calm me again. "Whoever it was, they weren't part of George's crew. It could just be someone that saw the bar opening back up. It could be anything. I can call the local precinct and have someone check the place out if you want. I don't know how to help other than that."

"Thanks, Kevin. That would be great. I'm sorry I keep bothering you. I feel like such a fool. I don't know how to be normal. I've never lived in the open like this."

"It'll take some adjusting; stop pushing so hard," Kevin reassured. "I'll call the station and see what they can do. Now get some rest."

"All right. Good night," I disconnected the call, and tossed my phone onto the table in front of me. It was going to be a long night. I could sense that sleep wasn't in my brain's plan for the evening, and even though I was going to be exhausted the next day, I grabbed a blanket and curled up in front of the TV.

oooooooooo

When morning came, I was not ready. I awoke with Mara standing an inch from my face giggling. I'd fallen asleep on the couch and cartoons now blared in the background as she inched closer and closer.

"Time to get up, Mommy," she giggled as she kissed my nose.

"Mommy's tired," I stretched and groaned as I shifted on the couch. All-nighters were not something that I was used to, and now I was going to be at work all day I'm sure.

"Can we have pancakes for breakfast?" She bounced on her toes as I sat up and wiped my hands across my face.

"Sure, baby. Go get dressed. Grandma's gonna be here soon," I stood and shuffled into the kitchen. As Mara disappeared into her room, I began grabbing everything I would need to make her favorite chocolate chip pancakes.

I was so lost in my preparations that when a knock sounded at the door, I almost jumped out of my skin. My heart thundered in my chest, and it took a minute for me to calm myself.

"Grandma!" Mara squealed as she blew past me and headed straight for the door. Before I could utter a word, she had it open and tugged my mother inside. "We're having pancakes. Want some?" Mara led her into the kitchen and then took off for the living area.

"Rough night?" My mom whispered as she glanced at me. "You look like you didn't sleep well."

"I'm fine," I muttered as I poured some of the batter onto the hot griddle.

"Don't lie to me, Sam," my mom pointed her finger at me as she scolded.

"Mom," I rolled my eyes. "I'm getting ready to open my own business. I'm back in a city that has more memories than I know what to with, and… I'm doing it all without *him*."

"You know Andy would have come if you asked." Mom lowered herself into a chair before glancing up at me.

"I know that. This was my decision, but please don't lecture me. I'm doing the best I can," I murmured.

"I'm sorry," she sighed before looking back toward Mara. "How's she doing?"

"What do you mean?" I flipped the pancakes and began grabbing plates out of the cupboard.

"She seems fine when we're together, but she's a lot like you. She keeps things inside. I just want to make sure she's happy," my mom offered a sad smile. "She needs people in her life other than the two of us."

"Mom," I groaned. "We've been through this. She goes to school. She's around kids there. She has us. Plenty of kids in this world grow up with only one parent. I want to find him, I do, but I don't know where to start. I thought coming here would help, but so far…" I waved in front me. "I can't live my life on hold. I need to move on and, hopefully, all of this will be a step in the right direction."

"Promise me that you're happy; that's all I'm asking. That you're happy, and she's happy," my mother smiled at me before turning toward Mara.

"I am," I nodded. "Breakfast!" I called as I began piling the plates with pancakes. I placed them on the table then poured milk for Mara and coffee for my mother and me. I was going to need it today. I was sure by the end of the night that I'd have no trouble sleeping at all.

ooooooooo

Once we'd finished our breakfast, Mom took Mara with her. She was going to drop her off at pre-School and run some errands. I wasn't sure when I'd be home tonight, so Mom had offered to let Mara stay the night. Things were going to be so much easier now.

As I placed the last dish in the dishwasher, I said a silent prayer thanking my mom for being so helpful. I wasn't sure why I was so surprised at her help, she had never told me no when I asked for something.

After locking the condo, I made my way downstairs to my car. The sun was high in the sky now, and the morning fog had burnt off. It looked like it was going to be a beautiful day, and I had a little extra bounce in my step despite my lack of sleep.

I was so lost in my own head that I didn't notice him at first, but once I closed my car door, I saw him. About a hundred feet away was the same figure from the night before. He was in jeans and straddling the same bike. A chill rushed through me as I quickly cranked my car. He was wearing a helmet so I couldn't see his face, but his posture didn't sit well with me. His bike roared to life as he twisted the clutch and took off, causing a cloud of smoke to rise in his wake.

"What the hell," I muttered as I put the car in gear and began driving toward the bar. This was not a coincidence. Whoever this was, he was following me. This didn't have anything to do with the bar. It was all me. Now that I didn't have Mara with me, anger had replaced the fear. I had grown up dealing with situations like this. This guy, whoever he was, was going to stop.

I pressed Kevin's number on my cell, put the phone on speaker, and tossed it in the seat beside me before heading to work.

"Hello? Sam?" his voice was cautious, I'm guessing, because our talk the night before.

"He's here," I growled. "This wasn't about the bar. He was fucking here, Kevin... at my condo."

"I'm on it," I could hear shuffling in the background as he put the phone down. "I'm on my way. Where are you?"

"In the car. I'm going to work," I snapped back. "Whoever this guy is... he's not stopping me. I'm not ever going back a life lived in hiding; do you hear me?"

"Sam," Kevin sighed, and I heard keys jingling. "Do you really think taking this person on is the right thing to do? You have Mara to think about."

"I'm well aware of the way things are," I pounded my fist on the steering wheel. "I said I'm not going back, and I'm not. Mara will not grow up like I did."

"I'm in my car now. I'll see you at the bar. Meet me around back," Kevin clicked off the line and my car went silent.

oooooooooo

When I arrived at work, Chris was already waiting for me. He'd volunteered to help check everything before we opened at four. Tiff was coming back to work tonight, but I wasn't expecting her until around three. The rest of my staff wasn't due in until three. Kevin was sitting in his car in a spot near the edge of the rear lot. This was the only guaranteed parking that the bar had. If you parked out front, it was on the street.

"Hey," Kevin lifted his hand in a wave. "Wanna talk in my car?"

"Can we go in? I've got some last minute things I want to check on before opening tonight," I motioned to the rear door.

"You can't be serious?" Kevin shook his head at me. "You've got someone following you, and you still plan to open?"

"I'm not hiding anymore. I want protection, not orders," I glared at him.

Kevin shook his head, "You are going to be the end of me. Why are you so stubborn?"

I shrugged, "Not sure. Maybe it's because of the way I grew up. I've never had a choice. Now I do."

"Fine," he sighed as he motioned for me to precede him.

Once inside, he began searching the place. I'm not sure what he thought he would find. Maybe it was just something that was a habit, and he didn't even know he was doing it. Satisfied that the place was secure, we sat in the corner booth I'd left covered in papers the night before. We talked for a while about all sorts of things. Kevin asked for a list of all the places I'd been over the last few weeks. He said that maybe this person was someone that I'd met who had formed an unhealthy attachment. "A stalker?" I rolled my eyes. Great, what else was going to crash into my life? Morning had come and gone, and as we talked, I soon began to relax.

"I'm going for a smoke break," Chris had waved at me as he disappeared through the kitchen.

I waved and then turned back to Kevin. I'm not sure what caused me to glance out the window, but when I did my mouth froze. He was there again. Across the street. "Kevin," I reached out and clamped my fingers over his forearm. I pointed at the window as I squeezed him to get his attention. "That's him!" I gasped.

Before I could stop him, Kevin stood and pointed a stern finger at me, "Stay put!" I nodded in acceptance and watched as he strode toward the door. He pushed it open and began walking across the street where the figure stood beside his bike. Kevin's hand was resting on his hip as he readied himself to draw his weapon. His shoulders were tense. I'd only seen him like this a few times.

When he reached the figure across the street, I saw him relax. His hand dropped away as he paused before reaching out the shake the man's hand. Their posture was friendly, not at all what I expected it to be. What the hell was going on? Kevin pointed at the bar as he talked to the man, before he turned back in my direction.

As Kevin made his way back to me, the guy on the bike shifted. He climbed on, cranked the engine, and shifted to face me more directly. It was as if he could see me staring through the glass. As he lifted his foot to the foot peg, his jacket fell open slightly, and I saw it…a badge. Right there, gleaming in the sunlight as it hung around his neck. He was a cop!

Chapter 5

As I stood motionless and watched the bike disappear down the street, Kevin came striding back over to the bar. He paused at the door, and his shoulders shook like he was laughing. Anger boiled in the pit of my stomach; nothing about this was funny.

"Well?" my voice was snarky but I couldn't help it. I was mad.

"He thought you were someone else. He said as soon as he saw the kid, he knew you weren't but his curiosity got the best of him," Kevin shrugged.

"And?" I rolled my eyes.

"And nothing. He won't bother you anymore and he apologizes." He shook his head as he began walking toward the back door. "Hey, Sam?" He paused before turning to face me.

"Yeah?" I stood and crossed my arms over my chest.

"I'm sorry that this is so hard. I am. I know that you had a rough childhood, and you don't want that for Mara. I want you to know that I'm proud of what you're doing here. I'll always help you... know that," he blew out a breath. "Promise me that you'll come to me the next time. Don't wait until you're scared. I'm here. I'll always come."

"Thanks, Kevin," I began walking across the room, and when I reached him I threw my arms around his neck. As I hugged him, I mumbled, "You're always there for me."

"It's not just a job anymore. I care about you like you're my own. I couldn't live with myself if something ever happened to you." He gave me a quick squeeze before stepping back. "I'm headed home. Call me if you need anything," he pointed at me like he was scolding me, but the smirk that slipped into place told me otherwise.

"I will and thanks again," I grinned.

"No problem. Good luck tonight," he turned and disappeared through the door.

I stood there looking around and taking everything in. I'd finally done it. I'd opened this place back up. I was a business owner, and I was going to be successful. I had to be, for Mara. We were going to thrive here. Chicago was full of possibilities, and I was more than ready to explore them.

oooooooooo

Opening night was a great success. Other than a few minor glitches, everyone seemed to fall into a rhythm. We worked like a well-oiled machine. Chris was a natural behind the bar, and as much as I enjoyed being able to wander around and socialize with customers, I found myself behind the bar most of the night. It was where I felt most at home, and the place was running smoothly enough that I didn't seem to be needed anywhere else.

We'd been open a week now. Kevin had stopped in once to say hi. He sat at the bar for a short time and then left. I wondered what he did when he was off duty. I didn't know much about him other than his career, and he was Dev's uncle. I felt bad. Did Kevin have a family? I didn't think so. If he did, they were very understanding.

Tiff and I had been running the bar the last few days. Chris had the night off, and as I surveyed the place, I couldn't help but smile. We were raking in the dough tonight, and the band I'd booked had brought a huge crowd.

"This is awesome!" Tiff screamed over the music. "They just keep coming and coming."

"I know, right? We're going be here late tonight," I laughed as I poured another drink. The doorman I'd hire was doing a great job managing the crowd. It was nice to be able to relax. I'd been worried, when I took over as owner, that I'd be spreading myself too thin. Tori was always a mess on busy nights. I don't think it was us that caused it either. I think she just lacked managerial skills. I hadn't done anything to learn them, but Mason, my doorman, seemed to think I was a natural.

"Wanna hang out after work? It's gonna take me hours to come down from this?" Tiff yelled as she slammed the cash register drawer shut.

"I guess. My mom has Mara for the weekend. They're having a camp-out in the living room," I laughed as I turned to get the next order.

"A camp-out?" Tiff's brow creased.

"Yeah… you know? They set up a tent inside. Mara wanted to go camping and I just don't have the time right now. Mom offered to take her on a camping trip this weekend at her apartment," I shrugged.

"Cool," Tiff tossed her head back in amusement.

I watched her as she worked with ease down at the far end of bar. I had worried when we first talked about her working here that it would be awkward, but it wasn't. Tiff and I had always meshed well, and tonight was proof. She manned one end, and I the other. We didn't get in each other's way and kept the flow of customers constantly moving.

"Can I get some service," a deep voice resonated from my left.

"Just a minute," I held up a finger as I continued to count change. When I turned to face the direction of the voice, my entire world froze. It was him, the guy who'd been following me. "What do you want?" I crossed my arms over my chest as I approached him.

"Whoa!" He held up his hands. "I just want a beer. What's with the hostility?"

"You scared the shit outta me for days and then disappeared. Now you walk in here like it's nothing. Who are you, and what the hell do you want with me?" I growled.

"Slow down," he sighed and rubbed a hand down his face.

Now that I had the chance to look at him, I mean really look, I knew that he seemed familiar. I didn't know why, but I could swear I knew him. His frame was tall and lean. His T-shirt hugged his shoulders just enough to show off the muscles beneath it. His brown hair was cropped fairly short, and when he stared at me, his blue eyes sparkled with mischief.

"A beer would be nice," he grinned as he held out a five pinching it between his thumb and index finger.

I turned quickly, grabbed the beer, and after opening it, I slid it toward him, "Two fifty," I called.

"You don't remember me, do you?" He smirked when I snatched the money from his grasp.

"Should I?" I quipped. I'd seen so many people come in this place over the last two weeks that I couldn't remember where I should know this guy from.

"We met briefly a long time ago, maybe four years, I think?" He scratched at his jaw as he stared at me.

"I don't know any cops," I grumbled.

"Yeah, you do," he laughed. "You know me," he shrugged as he lifted the bottle to his lips and tipped his head back.

"No," I shook my head and rolled my eyes, "I don't."

"Maybe this will help," he motioned for me to move closer, and as soon as I stopped in front of him, he grabbed my arm.

"Hey!" I tried to back away from him, but his grip was firm. He didn't have the menacing look that I would have expected, but more of a playful one.

"Relax. I want to show you something," he released me and stretched his arm out on the bar, palm up. "See that," he pointed to his wrist. "Know who I am now?"

"Shit!" I hissed. He was pointing to a tattoo, the same tattoo that Dev had gotten back when I knew him as Brian. "You're a cop!"

"Un huh," he nodded as he moved his arm from its resting place. He hunched himself back over the bar and began twirling his bottle with his fingers.

"But I thought," I shook my head, and glanced around. The crowd that had been present had dwindled to a small group.

"He said that he told you about me," the guy mumbled, and I started wracking my brain to figure how I knew him.

"Wait! Max?" I leaned in and whispered as I watched him tense. "Is that how I know you? Is that who you are?"

"I was," he huffed. "Not anymore."

"Ok," I turned my back on him as I tried to put the pieces together. "He told me that you were undercover, too, but he never told me your name. You look nothing Max did. Max had longer hair, and you..."

"I changed my appearance for the job," he muttered. "Sometimes we have to be somebody that we don't like very much."

"So why have you been following me?" I narrowed my eyes on him.

"I wasn't sure it was you. When I figured out that it was, I wanted to tell you how sorry I was. I know I skeeved you out back then. I had to say some pretty bad stuff to you," he sipped his beer, and looked away briefly. "He loves you, you know?"

"Dev?" My voice trembled just mentioning him.

"Mmm... he didn't want to leave you, but duty called," he sighed.

"Can I ask you something?" I bit my lip as I watched him nod. "What's your name?"

He smirked as he looked at me, "Jase. Detective Jase Stevenson."

"Nice to meet you, I'm Sam," I held out my hand. "I like this better than Max," I giggled. "This version is nicer."

"Go ahead," he looked away and sighed.

"Excuse me?" I wiped my hands on my jeans as I studied him. He seemed almost broken as he sat there.

"Ask me where he is; I know you want to," he mumbled.

"Why?" I placed my arms on the bar and leaned in closer. "You can't tell me, can you?"

"No, I can't. He's on the job. He has been for the last year. We don't get to talk much unless it's the middle of the night, or he's checking in."

"Wait, what?" I shook my head.

"We're partners. Didn't you know that?" Jase sighed. "Of course, you didn't. Why would he tell you?"

"Can you get a message to him? Tell him I'm here? Please?" I leaned closer and begged.

"I can try. I can't promise you anything, though, know that," he dropped his head, and stared at his lap. "He'll come back when he can." Jase finished the beer before standing. He took a few steps away before glancing back at me. "She's his, isn't she. She looks just like him."

I sucked my lower lip into my mouth as I slowly nodded. "Don't tell him. Please, don't tell him," I whispered.

"I won't," Jase murmured. "See ya around, Sam," he waved as he headed for the door.

"Yeah, see ya," I murmured as I watched him shuffle through the door, and out onto the street. I watched him as he made his way across the street. He paused, and stared back as if he could see me through the glass before shoving his helmet on, and cranking the bike. It roared to life, and the tires squealed as he peeled out of his parking space. He'd looked sad sitting at the bar alone, and I secretly wondered if he missed Dev, too.

Chapter 6

Over the next the several weeks, Jase became a fixture in the bar. He never mentioned Dev again, and I refused to bring it up. I didn't want him to feel awkward when he was around me, so most of time we acted like complete strangers. Tiff waited on him more than I did, and sometimes I was slightly jealous of their budding friendship.

"He's a nice guy, you know?" Tiff nudged me in the side with her elbow.

"Who?" I mumbled as I continued to stare at my laptop screen. I was currently sitting at a corner table, trying to work on payroll. We weren't supposed to open for another hour, but

Tiff was already set up and Chris wasn't far behind.

"Duh," she rolled her eyes. "Jase. He feels bad about the way you two met," she slid onto the chair across from me.

"By all means," I shook my head as I watched her get comfortable.

"Thanks," she giggled. "Anyway," she crossed her arms and leaned back. "I think you two should talk. I think it'd be good to have someone around here in law enforcement that you can trust."

"Uh, I have Kevin if I need anything," I sighed and went back to staring at the numbers in front of me.

"Doesn't Kevin have other cases? How long do you think he can continue to help you? You're not in the program anymore, right? Tell me I'm right." She reached across the table and grabbed my wrist.

"Yes," I blew out a breath. "I'm not in the program anymore."

"Ok, then," she stood. "It's settled. Tonight after shift, you, me, Chris, and Jase are going to hang out."

"Tiff," I started to interrupt her, but she laughed and shook her head.

"Don't Tiff me. We're going to hang out. You're going to have a life outside of work and being a mommy. For once, act like you're thirty and not fifty," she giggled as she shuffled over to where Chris was setting up his station. "Right, Chris?"

"Huh?" his head snapped up.

"Tonight... group hangout night," Tiff called as she disappeared into the kitchen.

"Hell yeah!" Chris pumped his fist the air.

"Great," I grumbled. Maybe Jase would turn her down. Who was I kidding; no one turned Tiff down.

ooooooooo

That night was the first time I saw Jase smile. Tiff had been right, he felt bad about the way things had happened for me. I guess it's true what they say about undercover work; it slowly drains your soul until there's nothing left. Most cops didn't make it their life's work. They worked a few years and got out. I found out that night that Dev had been working as an undercover detective for more than three times the average length. He'd been looking for me for years. He'd told their captain that he wasn't stopping until he found me. The ironic part here is when he finally did find me; he couldn't get out. He was in the middle of the job, and it wasn't finished.

As the weeks ticked by and summer turned to fall, my friendship with Jase grew. Tiff was right; he was a nice guy. We weren't romantic in any way; it wasn't like that. I saw him as more of a brother. Growing up as an only child in hiding, I'd missed out on things like having someone to look out for me. Jase seemed to take on the role with gusto. I'd laugh at his antics at times. He'd be perched at the end of the bar just observing. I think it was the police officer in him. His eyes were constantly scanning the room. It reminded me of the times that Dev had taken me out. Back then, I didn't know he was a cop. I didn't know he was on the job when we were together, but the signs were there, and now that I had the knowledge, I could see it more clearly.

On different occasions, random men would hit on me. I was used to it. Between working here and Vegas, I'd had my share of grabby entitled men. I'd never had a problem in the past getting rid of the unwanted attention. Usually a glare or a quick snappy retort would send them running in the other direction. Jase didn't know this though, and the first time he saw it in action was comical.

It was late, almost closing time, when a group of young guys came into the bar. It was obvious that they'd been drinking somewhere else. They sauntered up and clumsily sat on the stools in front of me. I paused in my wiping and smiled. "What can I get you?"

"Got any more like you back there?" The one in the middle of the group smiled at me.

"Nope, sorry. Just me," I turned to toss the towel in the sink and that's when the show started.

I don't where they'd started their party, but they'd been over served. The one with the big mouth jumped the bar like a hurdle. He banded his arms around me, and whispered into my neck, "I'll take you, then." His voice was slurred, and he stumbled as I quickly spun in his arms.

"I don't think so," I shook my head as I opened my hand and grabbed his junk in my fist.

"Owww!" He howled as he released me, but I tightened my grip and twisted.

"If you guys know what's good for you, you'll take your friend here home and teach him how to hold his liquor," I growled as I looked over his shoulder at the group standing wide-eyed with their mouths gaping open. "Get the hell outta my bar," I shoved him away from me, and glanced up to see Jase cracking up at the end of the bar.

The group of guys bolted from the place like it was on fire, and I shook my head as I let the adrenaline that had coursed through my veins slow down. "Thanks for the help," I rolled my eyes at Jase with a sarcastic snap.

"Looked like you had it handled," he chuckled. He slowly shook his head and his shoulders continued to shake with silent laughter, "I wouldn't let them hurt you, but I did enjoy the show. Remind me to never piss you off."

"Deal," I laughed as I turned to grab the rag I'd thrown in the sink. "You gonna get outta here so I can lock up. I don't see a rush people coming anytime soon."

"Umm," Jase got quiet, and then I heard the barstool scrape across the wooden floor. "Sure," his voice didn't sound sure, he'd had something occupying his thoughts all night.

"Can you get the sign on your way out?" I still had my back to him as I straightened bottles.

"You got it," he called from the door.

I heard it open and the bell at the top ring. I turned toward the cash register and hit the "no sale" button to release the drawer. As I pulled the tray out, the bell on the door rang again alerting me that it had opened. Instinct caused me to reach under the counter for the baseball bat I kept hidden there, but when I lifted my head to see what had caused the bell to ring, my entire world started spinning.

"Oh my god!" I gasped as I released the bat and stumbled backward into the shelf behind me.

"Hi," he lifted his arms out to the side as he shrugged. "I came as soon as I knew you were here."

"What? How?" I shook my head as I stared at him. He looked nothing like he had the last time I'd seen him. His hair was longer, much longer. It was pulled back in a tie, but I'm sure it would touch his shoulders if I released it. The scruff on his jaw was almost a full beard. He slowly approached the bar as if he was trying to soothe a frightened animal.

"I've missed you so much," he whispered. "Sam?"

The way he said my name put me in motion. I don't remember my feet moving. I don't remember much of anything other than the feel of his arms as they wrapped around me. "It's you," I cried as I buried my face in his neck. I took a deep breath and savored the smell of his cologne. It was just like I remembered, woodsy with a hint of pure Dev. "I thought you were on a job?" I murmured into his chest.

"They wouldn't tell me anything." The tears that I'd been holding back for years began to spill.

"I was," he whispered. "We cracked the case two days ago. I've been debriefing at the station house."

"Why didn't anyone tell me? I've left messages there. They knew I was looking for you," I pushed back and paced away from him.

"They can't, baby," he sighed as he pulled out a stool and dropped down onto it. "Protocol. No one's allowed to say anything until everything's signed and the DA has everything they need. I haven't even been able to get a haircut yet," he smiled a pained smile as he watched me. "I'm sorry."

"Sorry?" I spun to face him. I was a mess. Hurt, confused, angry... they all swirled inside of me as my brain tried to catch up with my heart. I missed him so much. I'd thought this day would never come, but as I remembered my daughter at home, the anger rose. "Sorry for what? For never calling? Never coming to find me? Never checking in?" My voice rose higher and higher as I crossed my arms over my chest.

"Sam," his voice stayed quiet, almost defeated. "You know that I would've come after you if I could have. I loved you. I still do."

My heart cracked a little at his confession, but I barreled on, "I've been living with a broken heart for four years. I've been going through life pretending to be happy."

"I know," he shook his head and slowly stood. He didn't approach me like I thought he was going to. Instead, he turned toward the door.

"Where are you going?" I demanded. "You can't just leave."

"I was going to go get cleaned up at my place. You obviously need a little time," he stood there watching, waiting to see what I would do.

I shook my head and wiped at my eyes, "How do you know anything about what I need? You don't know me, not the real me."

"I know enough," he mumbled. "Get some rest tonight. I'll come by tomorrow. We can talk. Figure out where we go from here."

"Dev?" My voice was timid, not angry like before.

"I know," he sighed and reached for the door he'd entered moments ago. "Believe me, I know."

"Promise me you're coming back," I was grasping at straws, afraid that if I let him go he'd disappear just like last time.

"I promise," he quickly strode over to where I was standing and leaned in. "I'm never leaving you again," he placed a light kiss on my forehead.

I closed my eyes and savored the moment. Blood rushed to the spot, causing it to tingle when he pulled away.

"Tomorrow," he whispered as he backed up and disappeared into the night.

Chapter 7

When I got back to my condo that night, I quietly crept inside. My mom was sitting in a chair in the living room reading a book. She yawned, wiped at her eyes as she closed it, and looked up at me. I must have looked pretty bad. Her eyes flashed as a small gasp escaped her lips.

"Sam! What's wrong?" She pushed to her feet and rushed over to me.

I stood there frozen, trying to put the events of the night into words. I wasn't even sure where to start. Dev showing up had been a complete surprise, and even though I'd been praying for this day to come, I didn't know how to proceed.

"Sam?" She pulled back from the hug she had me wrapped in and narrowed her eyes. "Talk to me. Did something happen? Is everyone ok? Is it Andy?"

"He came back," I mumbled as I felt my legs weaken under me, causing me to collapse on the sofa nearby. "He…" I pinched my eyes shut. I could hear my voice, but it sounded far away. It was as if I was talking, but it wasn't me at the same time.

"Who?" My mother sat down beside me and waited patiently for me to continue.

"Dev," I let the name slip from my lips. It was as if I was in a daze. "He came to the bar tonight."

"Oh honey," my mom wrapped an arm around my shoulders and tugged me toward her. I went willingly and let my head rest in her lap. She began running her fingers through my hair as she tried to soothe me. "This is good. I promise," she murmured.

I don't remember much else about our conversation. It was more of her talking and me listening. Sometime in the late hours of the night, I fell asleep right there, curled against her. It was as if I was five years old again, and she was comforting me from a nightmare. When I woke the next morning, a blanket lay over me and my mom was cooking breakfast in my kitchen. I yawned as I pushed myself up. "You don't have to cook," I called as I shuffled in on a mission for coffee.

"I don't mind," she grinned at me. "Mara's still asleep. Why don't you get shower before she wakes?"

"Sounds like a great idea," I wrinkled my nose as I glanced down at my smelly work shirt. It was rumpled and smelled like the bar. I'd been so shocked last night that I'd done nothing to prepare for bed. Beer and sticky mixers still coated my arms, and yesterday's makeup was crusted around my eyes. "Yeah, a shower sounds great. Thanks," I tossed my hand in the air as I turned for the bathroom. I tugged the tie out of my hair just as I stepped through the doorway and saw my reflection in the mirror. "Oh my god! I look terrible," I muttered.

"Mommy?" Mara's voice sounded from behind me causing me to jump.

My hand flew to my chest as I whirled around, "You scared me!" I gasped.

"Sorry," she giggled. "I missed you."

"I missed you too, baby," I leaned down and pressed a kiss to the top of her head.

"Eww!" she curled her lip. "You smell yucky."

"I know," I laughed. "I'm going to take a quick shower. Why don't you go watch some cartoons? Grandma's making breakfast."

"Yipee!" she squealed as she bounded toward the living room.

I sagged against the door as I gathered my thoughts and proceeded to turn on the shower. As I climbed in, thoughts of Dev and Mara clouded my brain. How was I ever going to talk to him about her? How was I going to tell her about him? What would I do if he didn't want her? How were they both going to react? I knew that I needed to reconnect with him first before I brought up the idea of being a father to him. We needed to do this slow, get all our cards on the table, open the locks on all those secret places, and really be honest with one another. That was the key here… honesty.

oooooooooo

"So what are your plans today?" My mom sat waiting patiently for me to answer. Mara had finished her breakfast and was currently giggling at some cartoon on the TV.

"I'm supposed to meet him at the bar this afternoon to talk. I have to get ready for tonight, so I'm assuming he's going to stop by before we open." I lifted my coffee cup to my lips and took a small sip.

"And then what?" she pressed.

"I don't know," I huffed.

"You don't know?" My mom's voice was tight. I could tell she was holding her emotions back, but I wasn't ready to get into an argument with her about Dev, especially with Mara in the next room.

I leaned back and tossed my arms in the air, "Tell me mother, what should I do? This is all new to me."

"He needs to know," she gritted her teeth and slowly shook her head. "You need to tell him and soon."

"I know that," I stressed the words. "We've talked all of ten minutes. I can't just drop this bomb on him. What am I supposed to do? Walk up to him and say where have you been, oh and by the way... you have a kid? I can't do that."

"That's not what I mean, and you know it," she sighed as she pushed her chair back. She glanced into the family room where Mara was absorbed in the TV show she was watching, "You need to tell him for her sake. She's young enough to forgive you for lying to her. Whether he wants her or not, he needs to know."

"I'll tell him, just not yet," I placed my arms on the table and dropped my head down onto them. "I need to figure out where we're going from here. I don't know if he even wants to be with me," my voice was muffled as I kept my head down. "Can you watch her today? I need to figure out where we stand before I take her along. I just…" I paused. I couldn't continue. My head was filling with too many 'what ifs' and I couldn't make it stop.

"Yes, she can come home with me. I'll take her to pre-school, and then take her to my place," she shook her head and laughed humorlessly. "You have to come get her tonight, though. You're supposed to be home early today. She needs time with you. I love my granddaughter, but she needs time with her mom."

"Deal. I'll be home for dinner. In fact, I'll bring dinner to you," I smiled before glancing back to where Mara was still perched. "Hey, Mara?"

"Yes, Mommy?" She bounced on the couch before turning around to look at me.

"Go get your shoes on. Grandma's going to take you to school. I'll get pizza tonight when I pick you up. Sound good?"

"Yea!" She scurried down the hallway. "Pizza!" I heard her cheer as she disappeared into her room.

Smiling, I stood and began heading to my room to get ready. Thoughts of Dev swirled in my head, and I tried to push them away. It was going to be a long, draining day; I could sense it.

oooooooooo

When I arrived at the bar, it was empty and dark. This was normal for eleven in the morning. I didn't have lunch hours, and that was working out great. We'd been packed every night since the place opened, and I wasn't seeing the need for afternoon hours.

I'd told Chris and Tiff that I'd do inventory today. I knew they needed a break, and they'd earned it. It also helped that this was my old chore. Tiff knew from the old days that I could do this with my eyes closed. She had tried to offer help, so had Chris. He'd given me some excuse about how I was the boss, and the boss didn't do that kinda work. I'd brushed him off and told him to enjoy his time off. It wouldn't come very often. He'd grinned and agreed.

Now, thirty minutes into this and half-empty bottles surrounded me. My knack for organization was driving me nuts. I was the only one that saw the need to have a place for everything. They all put the bottles wherever they wanted. I had certain places for everything, and tonight I was going to have a talk with them about it.

I leaned over to grab the crate off the floor just as a knock sounded on the glass of the front door. I paused and gathered my thoughts. I knew it was him, but for some reason, I was still surprised. When I lifted my head, he had his hands cupped around his eyes as he peered through the glass. It brought a smile to my lips just knowing that he was really here.

I placed the crate on the bar and shuffled over to the door. After popping the locks open, I opened the door, and stepped back to let him enter. "I didn't think you'd really come back," I murmured.

He stopped in his tracks, momentarily stunned, I guess. A look of hurt washed over his face. "Do you really have that little faith in me?"

I shrugged, "I don't know."

"Sam," he sighed as he pinched the bridge of his nose.

"What?" I tossed my arms in the air. "I don't know you. I have no idea who I'm talking to right now. Dev or Brian. Who is Dev? I only know seventeen year old Dev, not you." I turned to walk back to where I'd left my crate, but as soon as I passed him, he reached out and grabbed my arm.

His fingers wrapped around my elbow and gripped just tight enough to stop my movement. I could feel his body heat as he moved closer to me. His voice was harsh as his breath feathered across my neck, "You know me. I've always been me with you."

I shivered at his proximity, but held my resolve, "We were both pretending to be other people. You may think I know you, but I know you don't know me." I turned my head and glared daggers at him. His fingers released their hold on me, and he stepped back as if my words had slapped him.

"I'm sorry," he muttered. He rubbed his now clean-shaven jaw before removing his leather jacket. "I can't go back. I know that, but I'd really like to go forward with you. Can we do that? Can you do that?"

"What exactly do you mean? Friends? What?" I turned away from him and took a few deep breaths as I waited for him to answer. I knew what I wanted him to say, but I didn't know if he still felt it.

"Can you look at me please? I don't want to have this discussion with the back of your head," I could hear him moving around, and then the telltale sign of a barstool sliding across the floor.

"No," I grumbled as I leaned over to grab another liquor bottle. We stayed there in silence as I picked up countless bottles, checking the levels as he watched. I don't know what we thought we were doing... avoiding each other... trying to see who would hold out longer? Dev finally gave in when he saw me place the last bottle on the shelf.

"Sam, you're being ridiculous. Talk to me," he growled as he slapped his hands down on the bar.

"What do you want me to say?" I turned to face him, and at that moment, it all came pouring out of me. "I'm mad at you!" I pointed at him. "You promised you'd find me! You didn't! I've been living in Vegas for four years waiting for you! I stayed put so you could find me! Kept the same name all four years! Worked the same job! I did everything I could to make it easy for you!" My body was shaking at this point. Tears streamed down my face as my chest heaved with sobs.

"I tried," his face twisted in pain. "I tried for weeks to find you," he shook his head as his shoulders dropped. "I thought I had at one point, but then I got assigned to a new case. I was in deep. No one knew where I was except my handler. Even Jase was out of the loop," his expression begged for understanding, but I didn't care. I was angry, and years of hiding who I was began to pour out of me as I unleashed on him.

"You tried!" I screamed. "Not fucking good enough!" I grabbed a glass that was nearby and threw it in his direction. "I loved you," I began to cry as my knees weakened, and I slowly sank toward the floor. "I loved you so much. I would have done anything you asked."

"Sam, stop!" He shoved his stool back as he stood and raced around to where I was curled up on the floor. "We can fix this. I promise we can fix it." He skidded to a stop beside me and dropped down as he wrapped his arms around me.

I fisted his soft T-shirt as I buried my face in his chest and cried. "How? How are we going fix it?"

"I'm not on assignment right now," he whispered as he placed a kiss to the top of my head. "I'm going to stay here in Chicago and work. I'm going to take you out and fix us. I'm going to finish what we started years ago, and this time neither one of us is leaving."

"How am I supposed to believe that? You lie about who you are for a living. It's your job," I mumbled.

"I'm not going to lie to you," he soothed. "I promise. I'll do anything to fix this."

"Anything?" I tilted my head up and wiped the tears from my eyes.

"Anything," he nodded.

I picked up his hand and turned it over to look at his wrist. The skull and roses, where he'd inked himself to fit into George's group, were still there. He pulled his hand back and tugged his sleeve back down so it was covered.

"I've been meaning to get that removed," he grimaced when I peered up at him.

I nodded in acceptance as I stood. "Consequence of the job, huh?"

"I guess," he rose to his feet, too. "Listen," he gripped my chin. "I know it's gonna take time, but I want to see you again— outside of this place. When do you get off tonight?"

"I can't," I turned away. "I've already got plans tonight."

Dev's head snapped back as if I'd slapped him.

"Not a date," I clarified. "I promised a friend a girl's night." I knew that was only a partial truth, but with everything that had happened today, I wasn't ready to tell him he had a daughter.

"Tomorrow?" he smiled. "My place? I'll cook."

"I don't even know where your place is," I grinned. The easy banter that we'd once had was slowly coming back. The tension that had been radiating between us seemed to be evaporating.

"Yes, you do," he chuckled. "I haven't moved."

"Wait," I gasped. "You still have the loft?"

"Yeah, why?" He narrowed his eyes on me.

I couldn't tell him that we lived in the same building. I didn't want him showing up at my door. What if Mara answered it? "No reason, just curious." This new knowledge was something that I was relieved to have. I knew I'd need to be careful with my comings and goings. I didn't want Dev to know about Mara until I was ready. I needed him to be ready.

"So, tomorrow? Dinner? My place?" He cupped my chin and leaned in until his nose brushed mine.

"I don't know," I whispered. "I might have to work." It was a lame excuse, but he was so close that I couldn't get words out.

"I think you do know. I'm glad to see I still affect you," he smirked as he moved his mouth to the shell of my ear. "I'll be waiting for you." With that, he stepped back and removed all contact between us.

My body was strung tight with tension, and as he strode toward the door, I released a growl. "I'll get you back for this."

"I hope so," he chuckled as he shoved the door open and disappeared onto the street.

I stomped my foot as the door swung shut. This was so not fair. He still knew exactly what to do to wind me up, and as I thought about tomorrow night and our dinner, I secretly wondered if he had plans to help me remove the ache he'd created. I'd missed him so much, and now with the possibility of actually having him, I was feeling truly hopeful for the first time in a long time. All I needed to do was tell him about Mara.

Chapter 8

"You know this place will survive without you for one night?" Tiff laughed as she watched me scurry around my office.

"I know, but…" I stopped and sighed as I sat down. "I've never left anyone else in charge. It's not that I don't trust you guys, I just don't think I'll be able to relax knowing that the place is open and I'm not here."

"You can't live here," she rolled her eyes. "We've been open for a couple of months now; things are going great. Enjoy a night away," she grinned and then slowly pushed the door shut closing us inside. "The Bad Ass needs time with you to show you how sorry he is," she giggled as she watched me squirm.

I shook my head at her. I'd told Tiff all about the Brian/Dev saga that was my life. She knew the truth, and I felt like I could trust her. It was nice having another woman to talk to.

"We're only having dinner," I grumbled as I clicked away on the mouse. I was trying to submit the supply order before I left.

"Right," she chewed her lip. "Dinner at his place, alone," she giggled again. "I'm sure talking is exactly what he has planned."

"It doesn't matter what he has planned. It's what I have planned," I hit send on the email I was working on, and then closed the laptop. "Promise me that you'll call as soon as trouble arises," I pointed at her.

"I will, but you need to trust your staff. You hired me because I'm good at my job. Trust me; we'll be fine," she opened the door and began walking away. "Besides," she called over her shoulder "Jase is coming by. He can help if there's an issue."

"Wait, what? How can Jase help?" I rushed after her.

"If we have a problem, I'm sure it will be with some rowdy person. He can help," she shrugged as if it was the simplest thing in the world.

"You two getting close?" I leaned closer to her ear and whispered.

"I want to," she frowned, "but he's holding back. I don't know why."

"Give it time," I groaned. "These boys are full of secrets. If he's hiding something, it's because of the job. Trust me."

"That's what I'm afraid of," she muttered. "Hey, what are you still doing here? Go see your man."

"I am," I laughed. "I'm leaving right now. Happy?"

"Very," she giggled, "and I want details tomorrow."

"Not a chance!" I tossed my head back in laughter.

oooooooooo

I'd yet to tell Dev where I lived, so getting to his loft undetected was no easy feat. When I'd gotten back home that afternoon, there was no sign of his bike. I didn't know what kinda car he had, but I was sure he owned one. Chicago was not the place to ride a bike in the winter. With fall here, and winter approaching, I knew his mode of transportation would soon be changing.

After showering, I'd spent quite a while standing in my closet trying to decide what to wear. I wasn't sure what tonight was really about. Were we really just going to talk? Did he have other plans? Things had escalated so fast the last time that I wasn't sure how to approach the subject. My body craved the attention that he could give, but my heart was still hurting. I also knew that I couldn't keep Mara hidden forever. My mom was right; he needed to know.

After finally deciding on a soft cotton dress, I moved to my dresser and began trying to decide on underwear. Was tonight going to be about comfort, or sex appeal? I wanted to be prepared for anything, but I also didn't want to come across as desperate. Finally, deciding not to over think it, I grabbed a white lacy matching bra and panty set. I could still feel good about myself even if he wasn't going to see it. Right?

I quickly dressed and went to work fixing my hair and putting on some light makeup. I knew we weren't going out, and I really didn't feel like over doing it. This was different for me. I wanted to be Sam tonight, not Mallory, or Emily, or anybody else, just me.

I slipped on a pair of sandals, grabbed my purse and keys, and strode out the door. I lifted my chin in confidence as I stepped into the elevator. I needed to go up to the fifth floor. I lived on the third, and I knew once that secret was revealed, Dev wouldn't be happy that I'd kept it from him.

When the elevator stopped, I took several deep breaths before stepping out. The hallway looked the same with newer paint, and as I made my way to his door, everything began coming back. Being here, in his place, all the memories that went along with it peppered me from every angle.

I stepped in front of the door and lifted my hand to knock. Before I could, the door swung open, and I stepped back, stunned.

"I heard the lift," he smiled as he raked his eyes down my form.

"Uh," my mouth hung open as I tried to process everything. He was standing there in a pair of jeans and a snug T-shirt. His feet were bare, and as I let my eyes drag upward, I noticed he'd cut his hair. "Can I—can I come in?" I stuttered.

He stepped back and waved his arm toward the entrance as his lips turned upward. He appraised me as I stepped past him, and I couldn't help but feel his stare burn my skin.

"I didn't think you'd show," he chuckled.

"Why's that?" I mumbled as I glanced around the loft. It looked the same. Nothing had changed in the four years I'd been gone. The furniture was still a sleek modern look, the only difference were photos. Everywhere I looked, pictures covered the surfaces. His parents and family back in New York, and even... me. "Oh my god!" I gasped as I rushed over to a small end table. "I can't believe you have this."

He nodded as he watched me. "I've have others, too. I just like that one the best," I could hear him closing the door, and within seconds he was standing behind me. "I loved you, even back then." He plucked the frame from my fingertips and placed it back on the table. "I saved them all; I just couldn't have them out before. Rule number one of the job: no personal items."

"But now?" I turned to face him.

"I told you. I'm not undercover. I'm staying here with you," his eyes twinkled as he watched me process the information once again.

"Sam," he placed his hands on my shoulders. "I'm willing to do whatever I have to do to fix this. I love you. I always have. I want to be us again without all the secrets. I'll tell you anything you want to know, but first," he leaned down next to my ear, "Let's eat," he smirked as he backed away from me.

My breathing hitched as he chuckled and made his way toward the kitchen. Watching him, I growled in frustration. He seemed so natural standing there. I wasn't sure what it was, but seeing a man cooking barefoot was something that twisted my insides in the most delicious way.

"So what are we having?" I tried for nonchalance as I fought with my heart rate, trying to slow it.

"Pasta," he grinned as he looked back at me. "You okay with that?"

"Sounds great," I mumbled, sitting down at the table. I continued to dart my eyes around the room. It was weird. Everything was the same, but different at the same time.

"What's wrong?" Dev's brow furrowed as he carried the bowl of fresh pasta with tomato sauce over to the table and sat down.

"Nothing," I slowly shook my head. "I guess I'm just trying to take it all in. Being back here is weird for me."

"How so?" He scooped the spaghetti onto our plates and then went to work opening a bottle of wine.

"I don't know exactly. It's like we're here in someone else's apartment. I mean… I know it's yours, but it doesn't feel that way," I shrugged and began poking my fork at a noodle.

"No, I know what you mean. I've spent half my life pretending to be someone else. I like being me for a change, but I got this place when I was someone else. I'm still trying to make it mine," he looked around before he lifted his wine glass toward me. "To us," he winked and nodded at me to pick up my glass.

My head bobbed slowly as I forced air into my lungs, "To us." I took a sip of wine and leaned back in my chair. "Dev?" I sucked my lip into my mouth and began twisting my hands in my lap.

"Yeah?" He placed his fork beside his plate as he waited for me to continue.

"Is there an *us*? I mean, what exactly are we doing?" His eyes flashed for a moment before he sucked in a deep breath.

"Do you want there to be?" He crossed his arms over his chest. "What happens between us is up to you. I've told you how I feel. That hasn't changed," he squeezed his eyes shut and released a deep breath. "I'll wait until you're ready, but I need to know what you want."

"There's so much you don't know about me. Things that have happened since I left. Things that I've done. Things that happened between New York and Chicago. Things that happened after I left Chicago." I could feel my throat tightening with the sign of tears, but I refused to cry anymore. I'd cried over this enough to last a lifetime.

"Come here," he stood and offered his hand. I took it willingly and let him lead me over to the couch. He sat and pulled me into his lap. "I don't care about that stuff. There's nothing you could say that would change the way I feel about you," he wrapped his arms around my waist and placed a kiss on the side of my head. "I love you, Sam. I'll keep saying it for as long as you need to hear it, and it's the truth. I love you." He leaned in again, this time aiming for my cheek, but I turned my head right before his lips made contact and brought my mouth to his. It was tentative at first, light, almost a whisper of a kiss.

I held my head still while my hands lifted of their own to wrap around his neck. He groaned as my fingers wove into the soft strands. It was as if I'd ignited a fire. The embers that had been there waiting for fuel had found it. His body roared to life as his tongue parted my lips and dove in. His hands, resting on my hips, began to slide upward and caress my back. I collapsed into him, pressing my chest against his.

Our dinner long forgotten, he turned us and began lowering me onto my back. Our hands made sweeping motions across each other's bodies as we began re-learning the terrain. I could feel my back arching as he sprinkled my neck and chest with light kisses. "Sam," he groaned as his right hand began to work its way underneath the edge of my dress.

"Don't stop!" I panted. "Please, don't stop." I knew I sounded desperate, but I didn't care. I'd been waiting for this moment for four years. Worries that I'd had over our reunion began to evaporate as I watched him yank his shirt over his head. The chiseled chest that I'd missed so much came into view, causing my insides to tighten even more. I sighed when he leaned back down and pressed himself against me. It felt so good, and all I could think about was what was coming next.

Within minutes, Dev had us both naked on his couch. Our mouths were furiously blazing paths over the other's body. The muscles in his back bunched and twisted as he rocked himself against me. He was pressing into my thigh, but every few seconds he would rub right where I wanted him to be.

"I want you so fucking much right now," he groaned.

"What's stopping you?" I lifted a hand and cupped his cheek. He paused in his movement and briefly closed his eyes. "I want you, too."

"Sam," he dropped his head so his forehead was resting against mine.

"Say it again," I whispered. He peered up at me as if he wasn't sure what I meant. "My name... say it again," tears leaked from my eyes as I watched recognition dawn on him.

"Sam," he whispered as he connected our mouths once again, this time in a kiss filled with passion. When he pulled back, he trailed his fingers right along my hairline. "Do I need a condom?" He nuzzled my neck. "I'm clean, I swear. I got checked out when I came back from my last assignment."

I shook my head, "I'm on the pill. I trust you," I lifted my hips, and rubbed them against him.

"Shit!" he hissed. "You're gonna end me before we ever get started." He grabbed my hip with one hand and held me in place as he leaned down next to my ear and whispered, "I don't wanna come yet. When I do, I wanna be buried so far inside you that you can't think of anything else but me."

I gasped, and before I could respond, he rocked his hips forward and plunged himself inside me all the way to the hilt. My eyes rolled back in pleasure as a few mumbled curses slipped from my lips. Dev pulled back, but quickly slammed himself back in. "Oh fuck!" he hissed. "You're fucking perfect, Sam. Tell me you love me," his eyes bored into mine. "Tell me you're mine," he panted as he worked us closer to the edge.

"I love you. I'm yours," I cried as every muscle in my body twisted to the point of breaking, and then with one last pump of his hips, I shattered. My chest heaved as I tried to catch my breath. Dev continue to thrust into me with a speed I'd never felt before. His face held an expression I hadn't seen in a long time. Pure and utter love along with something else... fear maybe?

"Saaammmm," he groaned as he surged forward one last time, and then collapsed on top of me. His body trembled as he tried to slow his breathing. I could feel his cock twitching inside of me, and the reality of what we'd just done began to set in.

"What are we doing?" My voice was slightly panicked as I pushed on his shoulders.

"Baby?" His eyes widened as he leaned back to climb off me. "You're not sorry that happened are you? I mean, you wanted it too, right?"

I reached for my clothes, and began dressing, refusing to look at him. "I came here to figure things out. There's so much you don't know, and I don't even know how to begin to tell you," I growled more at myself than him.

"Whoa!" He reached for me and spun me to face him. "What are you talking about? Are you seeing someone or something like that?"

"No," I shook my head and wiped the tears from my eyes. "It's nothing like that."

"Then what?" His head tilted to the side as he appraised me.

"Don't do that," I scowled.

"Do what?" His forehead wrinkled as he watched me.

"Be a cop around me. Stop trying to figure out what I'm trying to say, and just listen to me," I huffed and began pacing.

"Okay," he stood and tugged on his jeans. "What is it?"

"Maybe you should sit down," My lips thinned as I watched him stare at me, confusion written all over his face.

This was it. This was my moment, and as much as I wanted to tell him, and knew I should, I chickened out. "I live downstairs," I blurted.

"Huh?" he shook his head.

"I live in a condo on the third floor. I bought it when I moved back here. I wanted to be close to you, and this place made me feel that way. So I bought a condo here," I rushed the words out as fast as I could and then paused as the silence enveloped us.

"And you thought I'd be upset about this?" He scratched his head.

"I didn't tell you. I thought you'd be mad about that," I shrugged. "I'm sorry."

He tried to keep a straight face, I could tell he was fighting it, but his lips slowly began to curl on the edges.

"So you're not mad," I bit my lip.

"No," he shook his head. "Anything else?"

I thought about Mara again, but shook my head no instead. "No, nothing else." It was a lie, and the fact that it was so easy to lie to him scared me. It was a byproduct of living as someone else my entire life. Lying was easy, and that scared me more than anything, but I just wasn't ready. I wasn't sure if I'd ever be.

Chapter 9

As I stood staring out the window, watching the city light up, Dev quietly stood behind me. We'd yet to go back to our dinner, which I'm sure was cold now.

"What are you thinking about?" he whispered as he wrapped his arms around my waist.

"Nothing," I mumbled. The truth was, Mara was at the front of my mind, but I couldn't tell him that. I knew it was going to be something that we had to discuss, and soon, but not tonight. Tonight, I just wanted to stay in our little bubble and ignore the outside world.

"That crease on your forehead, and the way you're grinding your teeth says otherwise," he leaned down and kissed my temple.

"Can you please stop," I sighed as I stepped out of his embrace and moved away from him. "I can't do this."

"Do what?" he reached up and gripped the back of his neck.

"This," I waved my arm between us. "You're analyzing everything I do. I just..." I growled in frustration. "Stop being a cop!"

"Sam," he let his chin drop to his chest as a breath escaped him. "I can't stop being who I am. I've always been a cop. I just don't have to hide it now. Don't you understand," he peered up at me before shaking his head, "I'm trying to be myself, to show you who I am. I don't know how to be anything else. Being a cop is in my blood. It's who I am."

"I'm sorry," I rubbed my eyes. "You're right. I want you to be you. No more hiding stuff."

"Want to finish eating?" he smirked at me. "I'm sure you're hungry."

"I guess..." my voice trailed off right as my stomach decided to growl.

"See?" he laughed. "You need to eat."

I gripped my middle, "That's so embarrassing," I muttered. "Yeah, let's eat," I made my way over to the table while Dev grabbed our plates and put them in the microwave. "So are you really back?" I watched him tense slightly. His back was to me, and I know he was trying to sound unaffected.

"For now," he sighed. "I don't plan on going back under, but I'm still a cop. I still have to work." His head turned slightly as he watched me out of the corner of his eye, "That's never gonna change."

I nodded as I crossed my legs. I knew he couldn't just quit, and as scared as I was about what the future held, I knew I couldn't ask him to change.

"Are you gonna be ok with that?" He carried our plates over to the table and sat down across from me.

"I'm gonna try," I muttered as I stuffed a bite of pasta in my mouth. "That's all I can promise right now. I'll try."

"I can live with that," he smiled as he, too, began eating.

When we were both finished, Dev gathered our plates and carried them to the kitchen. I started to stand, but he narrowed his eyes at me as he ordered me to relax.

"You cooked, it's only fair that I help with the dishes," I tilted my head to the side.

"Un huh," he waved his finger and made a tsking sound. "You clean up after people every day at work. Let someone take care of you for a change," he smirked and then turned back toward the sink. He had no idea how close to home he was actually hitting. I did clean up after someone daily, but it wasn't at work. It was a mere twenty or so feet below us.

"Well," I began to protest, but gave up when he glared at me once again. "Fine," I giggled as I stood and made my way back to the couch. I sat and glanced at my watch as I listened to the dishes clink together while he cleaned them. It was getting close to nine, and I was sure Mara was now asleep. I had told my mother that I wouldn't be out late, and now that Dev knew where I lived, I wasn't sure how I was going to escape without a million questions.

When he finished, Dev situated himself beside me and reached for the remote to the stereo. After turning on some soft music, he shifted to look at me. "What?" he smirked.

"This," I looked away from him as my voice dropped to a whisper. "It seems..." I trailed off.

"Domestic?" his voice strained, he leaned in and kissed my neck.

"Something like that," I stiffened when he slid closer.

"Sam, what's wrong?" he rubbed his palms down his thighs.

"Nothing," I sighed. "I'm just..." I wasn't sure what it was. Maybe it was the fact that it was all happening so fast again. Dev and I didn't seem to have a normal speed. Everything was always in fast forward. I couldn't explain why I was suddenly so tense around him. We'd already had sex. Maybe it was the fact that I was still hiding Mara. I just didn't want her to get hurt, and I knew that if I told Dev about her, and he didn't want her that's exactly what would happen... to both of us.

Without saying anything, he stood and offered his hand. I sat there confused as I stared at it.

"Dance with me?" His eyes softened as one side of his lips curled up in a boyish grin.

"Huh?" I watched him as I tried shoving my previous thoughts to the back of my mind.

"Come here," he tugged on my hand causing me to stand. As our chests pressed together, he wrapped one arm around my waist, and gripped my hand in the other. He placed our joined hands on his chest and began swaying to the music. Soft mellow guitar and piano chords began to float through the air as a man's voice began to sing about not giving up.

I could feel Dev's heartbeat thundering under our joined hands as he shuffled us around the living room. The music did nothing to muffle the conversation that was silently going on between us. My body hummed in appreciation as he caressed my back and leaned down to nuzzle my neck. "I've wanted things like this for so long. You don't know how badly. Since the moment I got you back here all those years ago, I prayed that I'd get another chance. I wanted what everyone has: a real relationship with the woman I loved, with no lies between us. I'm not giving up on that dream, Sam. Whatever it takes, I promise, I'm going to make it work."

I melted against him a little more with each word that tumbled softly out of his mouth. This wasn't the Dev that I'd found four years ago. Brian was an alpha, and this man... he was confusing the hell out of me. I wasn't complaining, but seeing this softer side was throwing me for a loop. I needed to him to boss me around. I needed to see that the person I'd met before was still in there. I wanted this one, but I wanted the other one, too.

I nodded my head as I placed it on his shoulder, "I want it to work so much; you have no idea how much." I wanted this for Mara. I wanted the happy family that I'd dreamed about as I grew up. I wanted Mara to have two parents that loved each other and weren't worrying about their future constantly.

"Stay," he whispered as the song ended. "I'll make sure you're up in the morning. Stay with me tonight," his warm breath trailed across my ear and neck causing me to shiver.

I lifted my head and stared into his dark eyes, "I can't." Hurt spread across his face as his eyes watched my expression for deception I'm sure. "My mom's back at my place waiting on me. I promised I'd be home tonight." It was a lame excuse and one I hoped he'd buy without asking a ton of questions.

His head bobbed quickly one time and his arms released their hold on me, "ok."

"Ok?" I wrinkled my forehead. "What? No third degree?"

"I trust you. If you need to go, go," his face appeared pained as if he was forcing the words out while trying to convince himself that it was the right thing to do.

"It's not that I don't want to be here, I do, believe that. I just—I have some things that I need to take care of before I can start staying over," I pushed up onto my tiptoes and placed a kiss to his cheek.

"Can I see you tomorrow?" He smiled as he trailed a knuckle down the side of my face.

"I think that can be arranged," I smiled as I turned and headed for the door.

As I gathered my things, Dev stood watching my every move. It was like he was memorizing this moment. I slowly opened the door and stepped out into hall before turning to offer one last goodbye. Dev watched me until I made it to the elevator. I heard his door click shut just as the elevator doors closed, taking me back downstairs to my place.

ooooooooo

Morning came too quick the next day. It was Sunday, the one day of the week that we were closed. I had promised my employees that Sundays would be their one guaranteed day off each week. I didn't need to be open every day. Business was great, and until that changed, I wanted to be able to make the bar a place people wanted to be.

Mara had woken before me, and I could hear her in the living room watching cartoons and giggling. I knew I needed to get up, but after the lack of sleep, I was really dragging. Even though I'd gotten home at a reasonable time, my mother had spent an hour lecturing me about the need to talk to Dev. Then, once I actually got to bed, I didn't get much sleep. I'd spent most of the night tossing and turning as I stared at the ceiling thinking about how I could tell him. One part of me said just blurt it out, while another part was afraid of blindsiding him. I think the worst part was that I knew my mom was right. Hiding Mara was not the way to go about this, and regardless of how he felt about me, he'd want to know his daughter.

As I laid there wrestling with the idea of getting up, my phone chimed with a text.

Mom: Running a little late. Be there in 10.

I flopped back on my pillow and released a sigh. Mom had agreed to go with us to the park today. The weather was supposed to be great, and with winter around the corner, I wanted to Mara to be able to play outside as much as possible. This was going to be her first time seeing snow. Winters in Nevada were much warmer. Chicago was going to be a brand new experience for her.

I quickly climbed out of bed, pulled my hair up into a tie, put on my slippers, and made my way toward the kitchen. Coffee was going to be my savior today, and I needed it fast.

"Morning, Mommy," Mara called as she bounced on the couch.

"Morning, baby," I smiled as shuffled into the kitchen. "Grandma's coming over soon so we can go to the park for family day today."

"Yeah!" Mara bounced again. "Can we have a picnic?" she grinned.

"We can stop at the sandwich shop and get something. I don't really have anything to pack here. Mommy needs to grocery shop," I gave her a fake pout as I reached for the creamer in the fridge.

"Ok," she giggled.

As I waited for the coffee to finish brewing, I leaned against the counter and watched my daughter. She looked so much like her father except for her hair. The blonde seemed to be darkening more each day. The light streaks that she'd had from the Nevada sun had almost faded away and had been replaced with a dark chocolate color.

I was so lost in my daydreams of the three of us as a family that I didn't even hear the knock on the door. "I'll get it," Mara squealed as she jumped up from the couch.

"No, I'll get it," I called as I rounded the corner and put my hand out to stop her. If I'd been paying attention to the time, I would have known that there was no way it could have been my mother, but my tired brain wasn't moving at its normal speed.

I yanked opened the door, and froze when I saw who was on the other side. "Hello," Mara's sweet voice was tentative as she stood behind me peering around my legs. "Who are you?"

With a drink tray holding two coffees in one hand and a small paper bag holding what was probably some type of breakfast in the other hand, Dev stood momentarily stunned.

"Shit!" I hissed under my breath.

He squatted down in front of Mara and smiled, "My name's Dev. Who are you?"

"I'm Mara," she giggled. "I live here." Her finger slipped into the corner of her mouth as she appraised him.

Dev's eyes lifted to meet mine, and a look I couldn't figure out slipped into place. He stood once again and held out the bag, "I brought breakfast. I thought I'd surprise you."

"I can explain," tears welled in my eyes. I knew what was about to happen, and I couldn't do a thing to stop it.

"Mara," I reached for my daughter's shoulder and turned her to face me. "Can you go play in your room? I need to talk to Dev for a minute."

She nodded as her eyes danced between us, "Sure, Mommy."

As a sigh escaped me, Mara took off running down the hallway. As soon as her door clicked shut, I turned to face the man in front of me.

"You have a right to be upset, but please let me explain," I motioned for him to come inside. As we made our way over to the kitchen table, a million different scenarios began running through my head, each one worse than the last. My secret was out, and now I was going to have to deal with the fallout. My baby was going to experience heartache in a way that I couldn't even prepare myself for. Dev's response to this, either way, was going to change our entire world.

Chapter 10

"I can explain," I was panicked and the words kept repeating as I watched him make his way into my kitchen. "I didn't think I'd ever find you; it's been so long."

His shoulders were tense, and as he placed the items he was carrying on the counter, he froze, his back to me.

"I'm sorry," my voice choked, and I sucked in a breath, willing the tears to stay hidden.

"Does she know?" his words were almost a growl. "Of course, she doesn't," he muttered more to himself than me. He turned to face me and lifted his arms as if he was willing me to make all of this make sense.

I slowly sank into a chair at the table and buried my head in my hands, "Please," I begged. "Please don't break her heart. If you don't want me anymore, that's fine," I swallowed as I forced myself to continue. I could feel my stomach churning, and I was fighting to stay calm. Mara was in her room, but if we got loud enough, she'd hear us. "She doesn't deserve anymore pain."

"What are you talking about?" Dev's voice was even as he shoved off the counter.

I slowly looked up and wiped at my eyes. "She doesn't know about you."

"I got that much from our meeting at the door," he crossed his arms over his chest.

"No," I shook my head. "There's so much more. So much I need to tell you… about Nevada."

"Is that where you've been," he shifted on his feet and pinched the bridge of his nose.

I nodded slowly and before I could speak, another knock sounded. My head snapped in the direction of the door, and Dev scowled. "It's my mom," I clarified. "We were going to have a family day at the park. Do you want to come?"

"Are you going to tell her who I am?" he questioned.

"In time," I whispered. When his scowl deepened, I continued. "You need to know the whole story. She's not going to understand. I need to tell you about Nevada."

He sighed as he closed his eyes and released a breath, "Fine."

"Fine, you'll come?" I stood up to let my mom in.

"Yeah," he followed behind me, and when I opened the door, my mother gasped.

"It's really you! You're back?" She smiled softly as she stepped into the condo.

"Yes, ma'am," Dev held out his hand to shake hers just as Mara came barreling out.

"Grandma!" she squealed. "We're going to the park… and we're going to get sandwiches… and Mommy has a new friend," her little mouth was moving so fast none of us could get a word in. "Right?" she turned toward me and grinned.

"Sure, baby. Go get your shoes on," I ran my hand through her soft hair before turning to face Dev, "I just need a minute to throw some clothes on."

After quickly dressing in a pair of jeans and a sweatshirt, I re-did my hair and placed a baseball cap on top of my head. My eyes were still red from breaking down in the kitchen, but I hoped the hat would help cover them. When I came back out into the living area, Dev and my mom were whispering to one another as they sat shoulder to shoulder on the couch.

"Ready?" I cleared my throat and watched them almost jump apart.

"Honey?" My mom glanced back at me and then at Dev. I slowly shook my head as I watched her face. I knew what she was going to say, and I mentally begged her not to. "I think I'm going to skip today. You two need time with Mara, and I've got lots to do at home."

"Mom," I warned.

"Really. I'll come next time," she smiled, and I could feel my breathing and heart rate speed up once again.

"Don't you want to be with me?" Mara's tiny voice sounded from behind us.

"Yes, sweet girl, I do, but I've got stuff to do. You and I can hang out after school this week when Mom's working. Sound good?" Mom stood before kneeling in front of Mara.

"Ok," she grinned before leaning over and wrapping her little arms around my mom's neck. "I'll see you tomorrow."

"That's right. You and I have a date to make cookies," my mom glanced at me once more before heading out the door and leaving the three of us alone.

"So are you still coming?" Mara stared at Dev.

"Sure am," I watched his face morph in front of me. Mara had him under her spell. I could see it. The anger that was there had melted away and wonder now filled its place.

"Come on Mommy, time's a wastin'," she rushed to the door and bounced on her toes.

"Ok, ok, I'm coming," I looked over at Dev one last time before following my little girl out into the hallway. Dev followed behind us, not saying a word. I could tell that Mara had him mesmerized. I silently wondered if he could see himself in her, I knew I could.

ooooooooo

We drove my car to the local park, and as soon as we got there, Mara took off for the playground. Dev and I trailed behind her in search of a place to sit and talk. Mara was at that age where she would make friends easily and just needed a watchful eye. Most days, we'd play together, but now, as I folded my legs under me at the base of a tree, I marveled at how independent she'd gotten.

"How old is she?" Dev broke the silence between us first, and I swallowed.

"So you want to do this now, huh?" I refused to look at him.

"Sam," he paused before he crossed his arms over his chest. "If she's mine I have a right to know her."

I slowly nodded, "I know you do. I'm sorry."

"You've said that, several times now," he huffed.

"She's three... she'll be four in April," I shifted, and brought my knees up to my chest. "I wasn't trying to keep her from you," I darted my eyes toward him and then glanced back at Mara. "I don't want her hurt. She doesn't know anything about you."

I could feel him stiffen beside me, "Why?"

I closed my eyes and released a sigh, "I didn't know if I'd ever see you again. I didn't know if she'd still be a baby if I did. She needed to have a dad."

"What are you trying to tell me?" Dev turned so he was facing me. He studied my face, and his eyes held a pain I had never seen before. "Is there someone else? Are you seeing someone right now?"

I shook my head slowly, "No," I swallowed, "but I was."

"In Nevada," he nodded in understanding.

"Yeah," I whispered. "When I moved there, I didn't know I was pregnant. I did all the things I'd always done when I had to move. I got a place to live, a job; I tried to start over... again." I blinked a few time as I felt tears resurface. I knew I wasn't telling him what he wanted to hear, but I had promised honesty and I was trying to keep my word. "I met Andy the day I started my job," I cringed when Dev shifted away. "I'm sorry. We didn't start out together," I shrugged. "He was my boss. He was nice. We worked well together and things just sort of escalated from there.

It was a natural progression, and when he found out I was pregnant, he stepped up. I didn't tell him anything about you. He knew the baby wasn't his. We hadn't gotten that far in our relationship yet. I told him the father didn't know. He was okay with that. When Mara came along, we moved in together. He treated Mara as his own," I sucked my lip into my mouth, and bit down on it.

"Where is he now?" Dev's voice was strained.

"In Vegas. I broke things off when I knew I was coming back here." I placed my head on my bent knee and began crying. "He was so heart broken," I sobbed. "He thought we had a future."

"Did you?" Dev reached out and slowly placed his arm around my shoulders.

I peered up at him, "No, I couldn't love him like that; I still loved you." I wiped at my eyes, "I stayed for her."

Dev's brow furrowed as he watched our daughter skip around the playground.

"She thinks he's her dad," I cried harder. "She thinks he didn't want her anymore. When we left, I told her it was an adventure. She asked about him for a while after we were settled. Now, she's stopped asking, but it breaks my heart a little more each day to have her cry for him. I know you probably hate me," I sniffed, "but please don't be mad at her. She needs a dad."

I watched his eyes soften as he listened to me plead with him. I could tell that his emotions were warring inside him, and I felt bad for the way I'd dumped all of this on him. "Say something," I begged.

"I," he pinched the bridge of his nose and swallowed hard. "I don't know what to say. When were you going to tell her about me?"

"I was waiting until we talked. I didn't want to tell her anything unless you wanted her. I didn't want to set her up for more heartbreak," I released a shuddering breath. "She deserves happiness. I don't want her childhood to be anything like mine was."

"You named her Mara," his lips curled into a lopsided smile, "after my mom."

"I did," my head bobbed when I returned the smile.

"Why?" he pleaded with me.

"Because she's yours. I wanted something to remember you by," I leaned to the side and placed my head on his shoulder.

"Mommy! Mommy! Mommy!" Mara came rushing at us at top speed causing Dev and me to shoot apart. She stood there for a moment, staring at us, before she shrugged her little shoulders and pointed at the slide. "Can you come help so I can go on the slide?"

Dev darted his eyes from me to her as he looked for clarification. "She can't go up there by herself. It's too high," I whispered.

"I heard that," Mara teased.

I started to stand, but Mara shook her head at me, "Not you," she scowled. "I want," she scratched her head like she was thinking, "What's your name again?" she pointed at Dev.

Shock covered his face as he looked from me to her, "Dev."

"Can you help me, Dev?" she smiled sweetly and watched him rise to his feet.

"Don't you want me?" I wrinkled my forehead.

"No," Mara shook her head. "Boys are stronger. He can pick me up easier," she giggled like it was common knowledge then took off for the slide. She paused after a few steps and turned to see if Dev was following, then she giggled again as he jogged after her. I watched them slow as they neared the playground, and my heart soared.

I'd been waiting for this moment for so long. Mara didn't know who her knight was, but seeing father and daughter play together was something I'd longed for over the years. Dev was a natural with her, and as she smiled up at him, I could see the hero worship all over her face. I leaned back against the tree and let the tears flow. I was tired of trying to hold them back, and as they coated my cheeks, I embraced them. This was it. This was what I'd been waiting for. I only hoped that it wouldn't be yanked away.

Chapter 11

After our day at the park, I didn't see Dev for three days. I didn't know if he was avoiding me, or if I'd just shocked him so much that he was trying to figure out what he wanted. I did know that he'd made an impression on Mara. She'd asked me numerous times when he was going to hang out with us again. I didn't have the heart to tell her that I didn't know. I wanted Dev to want to be with us, but I didn't want him to feel obligated to.

The bar had been running smoothly, and as the holidays loomed on the horizon, I was trying to figure out some new marketing techniques. Tiff had suggested having live music again. I wasn't even sure how to go about that, but Chris was in a band and had volunteered to be our house band while we figured it out.

"You sure this is a good idea?" I muttered to Tiff as I watched Chris set up the amp on the small stage in the back corner.

"Are you kidding me right now?" Tiff gasped as tossed her hands in the air. "You were here when Tori did this, right?" she asked sarcastically. "I mean... we couldn't move in here, it was so packed. The night we did this back when we opened went great."

"You're right," I slowly nodded as I let my shoulders relax. "I think I'm just worried that we're not going to be able to handle the business."

"We've got this," Tiff knocked into me playfully and grinned.

"Yeah, ok," I sighed and dropped down into a chair.

"Tell me what's really bothering you?" she pulled out the chair beside me and reached across the table, placing her hand lightly on top of mine. "Is it Dev?"

I peered up at her with what I'm sure looked like a 'duh face', "It's always about him."

"What did he do?" She sat there waiting patiently for me to spill it.

"It's more about what he didn't do. I told him about Mara. He spent the day with us and then disappeared. He hasn't been home when I have, and he hasn't tried to call me. I don't know what to think."

"Maybe he's working," she shrugged. "Jase hasn't been in here in over a week. Maybe they got a new case that they can't get away from."

"But why can't he at least call?" I huffed. "He wants me to tell Mara about him, but this is what I am afraid of. I don't want him to just disappear after she gets attached."

"I don't know what to tell you. Keep trying. Maybe he just needs time to adjust. Give him a few more days. Besides," she grinned, "your mom's got Mara tonight. We're going to have fun," she stood and shoved my shoulder lightly. "After we shut this place down tonight," she winked like she had this huge secret, and then leaned over, "you and I have a date with that bottle of tequila over there."

"Tiff," I rolled my eyes.

"Don't Tiff me," she leaned back shocked. "We haven't cut loose in forever. You don't have a reason to rush home, and we're going celebrate something tonight, whether it's this whole live music tanking or being a smashing success."

"You are…" I shook my head. "I don't have words for what you are."

"A great friend," she giggled before leaving me sitting there.

As the afternoon turned to evening, I forgot my troubles. I was really too busy to think about anything other than the task in front of me. Since Chris was playing tonight, I was going to take his spot behind the bar. It was second nature for me, and the more I relaxed, the more I forgot.

"We need to cut these then I think we're good," Tiff slammed a box of oranges and pineapple on the counter. "I hate cutting fruit. I always get sticky," she grumbled as she grabbed a knife.

"You always have something to complain about when it comes to this," I shook my head as I grabbed an orange. "I don't mind cutting them if you want to do one more sweep through the game room and make sure we're all set?"

"You don't have to tell me twice," she laughed as she bolted from her spot.

I chuckled as I watched her scurry across the room and disappear around the corner. I'd kept the pool tables and dart boards in the other room. They always brought a crowd, and after that long ago night that Dev and I'd spent here playing pool, I couldn't really make myself get rid of them. They held too many memories. Every time I looked at them, I pictured all the things he'd done to me on that pool table that night.

"We're all set up front," Mason, my doorman, called as he began walking toward me. "What kinda cover are you charging for the music?"

"Nothing tonight," I shrugged as I continued to cut fruit. "I want to see how well it does first. If we get too busy, I'll let you know and you can hold people at the door."

"Sounds good, boss," he nodded as he grabbed a bottled water out of the beer cooler. "I'll be taking a smoke break now. I'm not sure when I'll get another."

"Ten-four," I saluted him and giggled when he rolled his eyes at me. Even though I was the boss, I didn't rule over my employees. We had a good relationship, and they respected me, but I knew how to cut loose and have fun.

Later that evening, I laughed as I began thinking about how worried I'd been about the evening. We were anything but slow. The place was so packed you could barely move. Tiff and I were in a rhythm behind the bar, and time was flying by. The band had been a hit, and even though every available space was in use, I had a line around the block. I couldn't help the grin on my face. I wished my dad could see me now. He'd be so proud. I used to tell him stories about what my life was going to be like when we finally were able to be normal again. Owning a bar wasn't one of the fantasies, but running a business was. I knew somewhere he was looking down on me smiling.

"I told you this would happen," Tiff yelled from the far end. "What you've got is a gold mine."

"Yeah, yeah," I rolled my eyes. "You were right," I laughed as I served the next customer.

"You keep the crowds like this, and I'll forget you ever doubted me." She squeezed behind me and grabbed a beer. "This is insane; we're gonna be rich."

Seeing her smile and watching all the customers brought a grin to my face. We'd been successful since I'd opened, but nothing like this. She was right; I had a gold mine. Now I just needed to make sure that I could find the entertainment to keep it this way.

The hours breezed by as the crowd continued to gyrate to the heavy bass. I wasn't sure if it would ever slow down. My feet were killing me, and sweat trickled down my back and between my boobs. It had been a long time since I'd worked this hard. The temperature in the place also seemed to climb exponentially as the evening progressed. "It's fucking hot in here," Tiff screamed over the crowd. "Tell Mason to prop open the door."

"I'm hot, too," I yelled back at her. "The band's almost done with their set though. I think the crowd will thin down some after that. We're only open for another hour."

"I don't know about that," a deep voice sounded from behind me.

I spun, thinking that I might know the person, but the guy in front of me was not who I wanted it to be. "Do I know you?" I leaned against the bar.

"Not yet," he winked. "But you will."

"Pretty sure of yourself, huh?" I stood straighter. "What can I get you?"

"Well," he tapped his chin as a wicked grin spread across his face. "Since you're not on the menu, I'll take a Bud."

I closed my eyes and slowly let a breath escape me, "Coming right up."

"That's what they all say," he snickered.

"Excuse me," I scowled as I placed the beer in front of him.

He made a sweeping motion across the front of himself before looking back at me. He lifted the beer, took a sip, and then leaned closer, like he had a secret. "I'm already up," he took another sip, "and the only coming I want to do is with you."

I jerked back so fast I almost lost my footing, "Who the hell do you think you are?"

"I'm the band's manager, Josh," he winked again as he held his hand out for me to shake.

I groaned as I turned away from him. "Fucking great," I muttered. Chris hadn't told me he had a douche for a manager.

"Ok then," he laughed as he stuck his hand back in his pocket. "Thanks for the beer," he lifted it in a salute before turning to disappear into the crowd.

"What the hell was that," Tiff poked me in the shoulder.

"A real live dick," I huffed.

"Too bad," she sighed. "He's hot."

"Yeah, but he knows it. You should have heard him," I served the next customer as she watched me. "He thinks he's the shit. I'm sure he's a player, and with the band, he's always got girls around who are willing."

"Yeah... I know the type," she grumbled as she pushed away from me. "You better learn to get along with him, though, if you want to keep this kinda crowd; you're gonna have to put with that."

"Don't remind me," I reached for a towel and began wiping down the bar. In the last half hour, the crowd had thinned out considerably. The band was packing up their equipment, and patrons either had found a table to sit at, or had left. The place seemed deserted. It wasn't, but compared to what we had a mere hour ago, it felt like it.

"Last call," Tiff yelled over the jukebox that was now filling the place with recorded music. A few people got up, but most finished their drinks and began heading toward the doors. Mason was there, checking for Designated Drivers, and wishing everyone a safe trip home.

"Thanks," I waved at him as he closed the door behind the last customer.

"No problem; now hand me a beer," he grinned. "After tonight, I need one."

"Oh," Tiff made a pouty face and began talking in a baby voice, "Did Mason have a rough night?"

"You could say that," he chuckled as he snatched the beer that I'd just placed on the bar.

"What happened?" Tiff continued to taunt him, "Did you get hit on one too many times?" she batted her eyes as Mason's face began to redden. "That's it, isn't it?"

"Shut up!" he grumbled. "My girl doesn't understand that I don't see anyone but her."

"I think it's sweet that you worry like that," I smiled softly as I thought about how protective Dev was of me when he'd thought I was someone else.

"You and every other person in a relationship," he groaned. "Single girls don't get it. They see all this," he waved at his muscled chest, "and all they want is to try to catch my attention. When I tell them I'm with someone, they laugh and try harder."

"Sorry, buddy," I slapped his shoulder as he leaned against the bar. "I can't help you with that one."

He nodded and stood there for a few minutes sipping his beer. I was almost finished cleaning my section when I heard Josh's voice again. I cringed as he paused at the bar in front of me.

"Speaking of people who can't take a hint," I muttered as my gaze shifted toward Mason. He noticed and stood straighter as Josh laughed.

"Don't be like that," Josh smirked. "I wanted to talk contracts with you. We love this place and we'd like to make it more permanent."

"I'll have to talk to Chris," I forced a smile on my face. "He's one of my best bartenders. I can't let him off to perform regularly until I can find a replacement."

"You seemed to be doing just fine tonight," his eyes scanned up and down my legs causing me to cringe.

"I own this place," I snapped. "I can't be behind the bar every night. I was filling in tonight."

"Yeah," he smirked again. "You are good at filling things in."

"Can you stop," I growled. "I'm not interested, and you're just annoying. Desperate is not attractive on you."

"Whatever," he sighed. "I'm wearing you down. You'll see. By the end of all this," he waved his arms around. "I'll have you just where I want you."

"Not if I have anything to say about it," a voice rang out loud and demanding. I knew without looking up who it was, and my entire body buzzed with awareness.

"Who the fuck are you?" Josh turned to face the intruder.

"Her boyfriend," Dev crossed his arms over his chest as he stood in the doorway. "Who the fuck are you?"

Josh's demeanor changed right before my eyes. The cocky flirt was gone, and the business manager made an appearance. "I'm the band's manager." He turned to face me, "I've got to help them pack up. I'll be back to discuss logistics for continuing this arrangement."

I nodded silently as my eyes stayed connected with Dev's. Mason relaxed before excusing himself and leaving me there alone with Dev. I couldn't place the expression Dev wore, and as he continued to stare, I saw the domineering man I'd met all those years ago form right before my eyes.

"Where have you been the last few days?" I tried to sound annoyed, but after the exhausting night I'd had, I don't think I was very convincing.

"Working," his voice clipped, he strode over, shrugged out of his leather coat and tossed it up on the bar. Clipped to the waistband of his jeans, his badge gleamed in the low lights of the bar as he took a seat. His breathing was ragged, and the muscles of his neck were ticking with tension. "What the hell was that all about?"

"It's none of your business, but it was nothing," I crossed my arms and leaned back against the counter. "What are you doing here?"

"I came to talk to you," he gripped the back of his neck. "I needed time to process everything, and now I want to talk."

"Well, I've got plans tonight," I scowled. "You're gonna have to wait." If I wasn't so worked up over the whole Josh situation, I probably would have agreed to leave and talk with him, but right now, I was mad. I was mad that Dev had dropped off the Earth for three days without even a phone call, and now he wanted me to stop what I was doing for him. I was mad at Josh for being a pig, and was mad at myself for letting all of this bother me. "You're welcome to stay, but I'm getting drunk tonight." I tossed the towel I had in my hand on the back counter and rounded the bar. I untucked my Rusty Nail tee from my jeans and tossed my bottle opener on the bar as I began walking to the other side of the bar. We'd agreed to take a table over by the pool tables, and Tiff already had the tequila and a pitcher of beer sitting over there.

"Wait!" Dev growled as he reached out and grabbed my arm right above my elbow.

I snapped my head in his direction before glaring at his hand where it gripped me, "Let me go," I snarled.

His fingers loosened slightly, but he leaned closer to my ear, "I don't like the attitude you seem to have tonight. What's going on with you?"

"We haven't been together in four years," I smiled a fake smile. "You don't know anything about me anymore. You seem to think it's ok to come and go from my life whenever you feel like it. I'm growing rather tired of that," I pressed my lips together as I watched my words hit their mark.

He released me as hurt filled his eyes.

"You can stay, or go, I don't really care, but me and that bottle are going to be good friends in about five minutes," I turned and walked to the table, poured myself a shot, and tossed it back before making eye contact with him once again.

"Fuck it!" he growled as he marched over, yanked the bottle from my grip, and went mouth to mouth with it right there in front of me. "We're gonna talk, and you're gonna listen," he slammed the bottle down. "If I have to get shit faced with you, then fine," he leaned right next to my ear. "You can pretend you're mad at me all you want, but that tremor that runs through your body every time you're near me isn't as subtle as you think it is. You need me like I need you, and tonight I'm gonna prove it. If I have to tie you down to get you to listen to me, then I will." His teeth nipped at my ear before he backed up, grabbed the bottle, and chugged again. "Your turn," he smirked as he shoved it into my hands.

Oh, fuck! Brian was back, and as much as I loved my sweet Dev... I craved Brian like an addict craves their next hit.

Chapter 12

As we stood there glaring at each other, daring the other to move, Tiff and Chris rounded the corner laughing together. When they saw us, standing there in our stare down, they stopped and almost bumped into one another.

"Shit!" Tiff hissed as she darted her eyes between the two of us. "Hey, Sam?" she slowly approached me. "Everything okay?"

"I'm fine," I angled my head to the side as I took another swing of liquor. It burned its way down my throat, and Dev's eyes flared as he watched me. "Want some?" I held the bottle out toward her.

"Damn!" she glanced from the bottle to me, back to the bottle, and then to Dev. "That was fairly full when I set it there. You two better slow down."

"I'm fine. Chicago's finest is here to protect me apparently," I rolled my eyes, and the room shifted slightly. I was being a bitch, and I knew it. I just didn't care. Dev stiffened beside me before shaking his head.

"I'm not too keen on the idea, but I will throw you over my shoulder, and cart your ass out of here if I need to, Samantha," he growled as he leaned next to my ear. "Don't try my patience."

I shivered as I heard him snicker. This only fueled my anger. He was laughing at me, and all I seemed to be able to do was show him how much my body wanted him.

"We playing cards or what?" Chris broke the tension as he moved around us and took a seat at the table. He poured himself a beer and began shuffling the playing cards.

Tiff silently watched us as she took a seat beside him. Dev took the chair across from Tiff, turned it around backwards, and sank down straddling it. His head tipped back so he could meet my glare, and he smirked. "Sit down, Samantha," he pointed his chin at the chair beside him, "before I put you there."

Holy hell, where had this man been? My insides twisted as I tried to decide how much I wanted to push him. I liked this, no, make that loved this. This is the man I wanted, and the fact that my anger seemed to incite him made me want to make him mad more often.

I dropped down onto the chair with a sigh before turning to glare at him, "You can't tell me what to do."

"The fuck I can't," his eyes narrowed before they swept over my body.

"Enough with the sexual tension in here," Chris rolled his eyes as he began shuffling the cards. "You two need to go back in the office and take care of that."

"Do you like working here?" Tiff gasped as she turned to face Chris.

"Yeah," he nodded as he began dealing cards.

"Then I suggest you shut up," she hissed at him before winking at me. "I got your back, babe," she giggled. "If this one," she pointed at Dev "needs reminding of anything, I'll help."

Dev folded his arms on the table as he chuckled at Tiff's expression. She was going for stern, but she really did look funny. He ran his knuckles along his scruffy jaw as he sat there deep in thought. "Hmmm. Is this for money tonight?"

"Naaa. Just bragging rights," Chris picked up his cards to look at them, "but money's okay."

He must have gotten a good hand. I glanced at Dev, then Tiff. She was watching us, and I gave a slow nod showing that I was fine.

"Where's your partner?" Tiff blurted out. "He too good for this place now?"

Dev snickered, "He's sleeping. We've been up for two days straight doing surveillance. Trust me... he likes you. He wouldn't stay away on purpose."

"He sure has a funny way of showing it," Tiff muttered under her breath.

"Jase has issues. I mean we all do," he motioned to his chest, "but Jase's are some big ones. Give it time if you really like him."

Tiff shrugged, "I don't really know him. He doesn't like to talk about himself..."

"Like I said... he has issues. It's not my place to talk shit about him either," Dev scowled as he placed two cards in front of himself and took two more off the deck. "So," he turned to look at me "What do I get if I win?"

"You can keep that smug look you've got," I retorted and I refused to make eye contact. I didn't want him to see the lust that filled my eyes, or the way my cheeks were heating.

"I was thinking more along the lines of something tangible, like what I won when we played pool that time?" he smirked as he watched me fidget.

"I have no idea what you're talking about," I glared at my cards. I think, in my alcohol soaked brain, I was under the impression that if I stared at them long enough I could change them.

"You gonna play, or what?" Chris laughed as he watched me.

"Shut up!" I tossed my hand down. "I'm too wired for this," I stood and half stumbled, half shuffled over to the jukebox in the corner.

"Sit down before you hurt yourself," Dev demanded as he turned to face me.

"I'm not that drunk," I giggled as I pushed some buttons on it and waited for music to fill the air.

"I beg to differ," Dev sighed as he tossed his cards on the table, and dragged his palms down his face. "Sorry guys, I'm out," he stood, and as he approached me, all the other movement in the room seemed to fade away. I don't really know how long it took him. Probably only a few seconds, but as his body moved across the floor toward me, it felt like time had stopped. "You know," he whispered as he stopped right behind me. "You're making it really hard for me to be a gentleman tonight," his voice was ragged as he leaned down next to my ear.

"Maybe, I don't want a gentleman," I smiled sweetly up at him as I pushed another button on the jukebox causing the song to change. "Maybe I like this."

"Sam!" he hissed as he pressed his chest into my back. He turned us so his back was to our table, and his body blocked Tiff and Chris's view. One hand cupped my breast as the other snaked down the front of my body, cupping me through my jeans. He released a groan when I pushed my hips back into him. "I didn't come here for this," his breath drifted across my neck at barely a whisper.

"Why did you come here then," I panted, swaying to the music.

"I want to talk to you about Mara," he moved his hands to spin me so I was now facing him. "I needed to figure things out," his eyes softened. "I wanna be part of her life."

The sweet man from weeks ago was back, and as much as I loved him, he was killing my buzz. "Well, I'm not really in the mind set to talk about this right now," I huffed. "Can we table this until tomorrow? I'm off duty tonight. She's with my mom. I want to cut loose for once and not worry about the future."

"I can respect that," Dev nodded. His body was pressed against mine, and his hands were sitting lightly on my hips. We were barely moving, but it was enough to keep the tension humming right below the surface.

"We're gonna head out before you two start humping right in front of us," Tiff yelled and chairs began to scrape across the floor. "I'll lock up," she called again. Just as the door dinged open, I heard her snicker, "Use protection!"

"Shut up!" I yelled back without looking. Dev's chest shook with laughter as I let my chin drop. "Sometimes I hate her," I grumbled just as the song changed.

"What the hell is this?" Dev's confused tone caused me to start laughing.

"I like the older stuff. This is one of my favorites," I giggled and hiccupped at the same time just as an older Keith Sweat song filled the room.

"Seriously?" Dev's forehead creased as he stared at me. "Babe," he sighed, "I think you've had too much to drink."

"Have not!" I hiccupped again and stumbled at the same time. "You can leave, too, if you're going be like that." I pulled back out of his arms and forced a pout on my lips as I watched his eyes darken. I don't know what I did, but the beast under the surface was coming out to play once again.

"Samantha," he warned as he tightened his grip on my waist. "Don't argue with me," his eyes flared as his hands slipped down to cup my rear. He tugged me closer until we were touching from our knees to our chests and he pushed his hips forward so I could feel what I was doing to him. "Don't test me."

"Or what?" I nibbled my lips as I blinked my eyes up at him. I wanted to push him past the point of control. He was driving me nuts tonight, and I wanted to take him with me.

His eyes squeezed shut as a few muttered curses slipped from his lips. I barely had time to register what was happening before he leaned down and crashed into my mouth.

Our lips melded together like two pieces of a puzzle. His hands tightened their grip as I moaned into his mouth. Heaven, that's what it felt like in his arms. I had no other words to describe it. My body subconsciously leaned into him as his mouth slanted over mine. His tongue licked at my lips as one hand came up to cup the back of my head, pinning me to him.

"Dev?" I panted. "More," I gripped his shoulders to keep from melting as he continued to devour my mouth. My brain was failing when it came to words, but my body seemed to be having its own silent conversation with the man in front of me.

I tried to back up slightly. I wanted to go back into the office. There was a couch back there, and we could use it, but Dev had other plans. He pulled back, breaking the kiss as a wicked gleam flashed across his eyes. "I've got a better idea," he murmured against my lips. He lifted me as if I weighed nothing, sealed his mouth back over mine, and resumed the kiss as he spun us and began to stalk toward the pool table in the back. It was behind a half wall, and couldn't be seen from anywhere in the room. A few of our more serious players liked to use it because of the privacy.

"Dev?" I looked up him as he set me on the edge and took a step back.

"You're drunk," he gripped his neck and took a steadying breath. "Are you sure about this?"

Whoa, where had that come from? This man was going to send my emotions into a tailspin. One minute he was bossing me around, and the next he was asking permission. I grinned up at him as I slid off the edge of the pool table. "I don't know about you," my grin widened, "but right now," I unsnapped my jeans and shoved them down to my ankles, "I need to be fucked... hard!" I kicked my pants to the side, and reached for the waistband of my panties, "and if you can't do that for me, I'll find someone who can."

Before the last word completely fell from my lips, he pressed against me, "You like it when I boss you around?" he nipped at my ear. "Does that turn you on?" His fingers slipped between my legs and probed. "Fuck baby," he groaned.

"That's what I'm hoping for," I giggled before sobering. I reached for his belt buckle and began working it loose. "Now get out of these and show me what you're made of."

"Oh hell," he muttered as he shoved his jeans and boxers down to his knees. "Turn around," he spun me so I was facing the pool table. "Hang on," he placed my hands out in front of me, "and don't let go. If you do, I'm gonna stop," his voice was a warning as he pressed his thighs against my rear. When he pulled back, separating us for a few seconds, I almost whimpered. "You don't know what you're asking for," he muttered just as he rocked forward, slamming into me.

"Fuuuuuck!" he groaned, before pulling back and rocketing forward once again. I yelped at first, but the sensations that assailed me quickly replaced any shock. I had unleashed him, and as much as he'd tried to hold back in the beginning, he was now finally letting go.

"More," I panted. "Harder."

"I'm not gonna last," he gasped as I felt him swell inside of me.

"Don't hold back," I begged. "Please....don't ever hold back with me," my voice was desperate as I began to tremble. I could feel my orgasm right below the surface, and even in my inebriated state, I knew that I was close. "I'm close... more," I panted.

With a roar, he joined me, both our bodies trembling as we slumped over the pool table fighting to stay upright. Sweat trickled from my forehead and neck as I tried to slow my breathing. This was by far the most erotic encounter that we'd had, and I immediately felt the loss as he pulled himself from me and righted his clothes. "Now that's more like it," Dev's voice sounded hazy as my brain came back to the present.

"What's that?" I looked over my shoulder and found him staring at me.

"You, spread out like that, with evidence of me all over you," his eyes flared as he reached out and caressed my rear with his palm. "I like you just like this."

"Why don't you come to my place and we can do it again?" I challenged as I pushed myself up. "I've got the place to myself tonight."

He nodded, and without another word, I got dressed, locked up, and walked out to my car with Dev following behind me. All thoughts of talking about our future were in the back of my mind. I didn't want anything to bring me down from the high he'd put me in. All that mattered tonight was losing myself in Dev and our undeniable connection. We could figure out how he was going to fit in Mara's life and mine in the morning.

Chapter 13

When the sun began to filter through the blinds in my room alerting me of the hour, I groaned. Every muscle in my body ached, including my head. I'd had too much tequila last night, and I'd lost count of how many times Dev and I had had sex. The soreness between my thighs was a constant reminder, throbbing every time I moved. I still wasn't sure what had come over me, but as I snuggled under the covers of my bed, memories of the shower, couch, and wall infiltrated my hung-over head.

"Don't do that unless you plan to take care of it," Dev's sleepy voice rasped from behind me when I pressed into him.

"No," I grumbled. "No more. I think you broke me."

He chuckled as his arms wrapped around my middle and tugged me closer. "You weren't complaining last night," he nuzzled my neck and nipped my ear. "In fact," he paused, "you were begging for more."

"Minor lapse in judgment," I muttered as I pressed my hips back.

"Stop!" he hissed as he gripped my hip and held me in place. "I wasn't kidding."

"I have to get up," I sighed. "My mom will be bringing Mara home soon, and I don't want to still be in bed when that happens."

"Sam?" he tugged on my shoulder so I'd roll over to face him. "I meant what I said last night. I wanna be part of her life."

"I know," I mumbled. "I know you meant it, and I know you want to be a good dad, but..." I looked away.

"But what?" His forehead wrinkled, and I saw slight panic appear in his eyes. "I have a right to see her. You can't keep me away."

"It's gonna take time. She doesn't know you. She's only three. It's gonna be hard for her to understand," I leaned in and brushed my lips lightly across his. "We'll get there, but you have to trust me."

"I do," he murmured against my mouth.

If I'd been paying attention to my surroundings, I would have heard the door open, but Dev had a bad habit of distracting me. Whenever he was around, it seemed that nothing else registered in my realm. Little things that normally came naturally required work, and thinking became a chore.

"Mommy!" Mara squealed as the door to my bedroom flew open. Dev and I jumped apart like two teenagers caught by their parents. My mother laughed silently from the hallway as she stared at us.

"See you kids later," she called in an amused voice as she turned and left. She'd bolted so fast you would have thought she'd walked in on us actually doing it.

"Mara, honey, what are you doing?" I stammered as I watched her climb up on the bed. She bounced on her knees a few times, her little arms shrugging. Her eyes darted from me to Dev and back again before she began to crawl toward me.

"Why are you naked, Mommy?" She scrunched her little nose as she moved closer. "Are all your PJs dirty?"

I tugged the sheet up higher and wrapped it as close as I could get it. I was trapped along with Dev, and Mara didn't seem to want to leave us. Her questions were causing me to turn a bright red, and Dev just laughed silently. His shoulders were shaking harder and harder as he watched me flounder.

"I just woke up, baby. Can you go watch cartoons for a minute so I can get dressed?"

"Why's your friend here? Did you have a sleepover?" her little finger pointed at Dev, and then me. "You should wear PJs. What happened to your clothes?"

"Mara?" I rubbed her head with one hand as I tightened my grip on the sheet with the other. "You know how, at the old house, you had to knock before you came in my room?"

Her brow furrowed more as she continued to stare at Dev. "Yeah," she slowly nodded. "Daddy was there."

"Well, you gotta do that here, too," I hoped she was catching on, but based on her expression I'd only made it worse.

"But Daddy isn't here," she scratched her head, and I felt Dev stiffen beside me.

"Hey Mara," Dev caught her attention at just the right time. "You wanna go to the zoo today? I've got the day off. Maybe your mom and I can take ya."

"Really?" she bounced on her knees squashing all thoughts of Andy.

"Go watch some cartoons so we can get ready," he pointed to the bedroom door as Mara leaped from the bed and scurried out, slamming the door behind her.

As soon as the door closed, Dev threw back the sheet and swung his legs over the side of the bed. I sat there stunned by the whole turn in events, and just watched him. I was waiting for the anger and betrayal that I knew he was feeling to be unleashed, but it never came.

His bare back faced me as he tugged on his boxers and jeans. The strong dominating man that I'd spent the night with was gone, and as his shoulders dropped in defeat, I saw what my deception was truly doing to him.

"I'm sorry," I murmured. "She doesn't know."

"You have to tell her," he begged as he stood to face me. "I can't keep ignoring the fact that she's mine and she calls *him* Dad".

"I will. I promise," I wiped at my eyes as I felt them tear up. "Thank you," I glanced down at my lap, "for today. She loves the zoo."

"It's nothing. I loved it, too." He grabbed his T-shirt, slipped it on, and walked over to the bedroom door. "I'm gonna go home and get cleaned up. I'll be back in an hour, and we'll go, ok?"

"Sure," I murmured as I looked away. Watching him like this was killing me. Dev was going to be a great father.

"See ya later," he nodded before disappearing out into the living room.

I heard muffled voices coming through the door, but I couldn't understand what was being said. I figured he was giving Mara the same speech he'd given me. I'm sure she wondered why he was leaving, and when he'd come back. I only hoped that when I told her about him, he'd be around more.

ooooooooo

After buckling Mara into her car seat, Dev slipped into the driver's seat. He knew the roads better than I did, and my brain was too busy thinking about how to tell my daughter the man with us today was her father. Different scenarios had been running through my head all morning. Would she hate me when she knew the truth? I thought about the anger I'd felt for my father every time we'd moved when I was a child. I didn't realize then that it was for my safety and that he loved me more than anything in the world. That understanding didn't come into play until I became a parent myself. I wished my dad was here so I could tell him that I loved him and understood why he did what he did.

"What are you thinking about?" Dev glanced at me as he reached over and squeezed my knee.

"My parents, Mara, you…" I whispered. "How I'm gonna tell her."

He slowly nodded as he squeezed once again, "I'll help you; you know that, right? We can tell her together."

"Ok," I murmured as I turned my head to gaze out the window.

"Are we there yet?" Mara called from the backseat.

"Yep," Dev grinned as he turned into the parking lot.

In the distance, you could see two large stone elephants rearing up on their hind legs creating an arch. A giant sign with red lettering connected their trunks identifying the entrance to the zoo.

"Ooooh!" Mara gasped in wonder. We'd been to the zoo in Vegas, but never here. My mom had promised a trip a while back, but was never able to follow through. "It's so cool," she smiled as she started fidgeting in her car seat. "Let me out!"

"Hang on," I laughed as I watched her. I silently wished that there were still things in this world that amazed me the way they did her.

After parking near the entrance, Dev opened Mara's door and helped her out while I went around the front. We'd packed a lunch, but left it in the trunk while we explored. Dev had mentioned going back to the park later to eat. Mara had enjoyed it there, and he'd hoped that we could talk. I'd blanched at the idea, but it had gone unnoticed by my spunky daughter.

"Hurry up!" Mara reached for Dev's hand and tugged him after her as she began to skip toward the ticket booth.

"Three please," Dev removed his wallet from his back pocket and shoved a fifty toward the guy working the booth.

"You don't have to pay for us," I stumbled over my words as I began digging through my purse. "I can get ours."

Dev turned and his soft expression morphed into a stern one, "I take care of what's mine, Samantha."

My eyes widened as Mara giggled beside him, "Nobody calls Mommy that, except Grandma."

"Oh really?" An amused Dev chuckled as he led Mara to the entrance.

"Yeah. When Grandma's mad at her, she calls her that. Are you mad at her?" Mara peered up at him waiting for an answer.

I watched Dev stare at her like he'd didn't understand her question. He looked back where I was following him, and I smirked. I knew he didn't know how to respond to her question, and I wanted to watch him flounder for a bit. It served him right trying to put me in my place like that.

"Yeah, Dev," I grinned as I sidled up beside him, "am I in trouble?"

His nostrils flared and his voice lowered to a deep rasp. "Don't test me," he warned. "Just because she's here doesn't mean you're safe."

I shivered and tugged my coat tighter around my body. I didn't want to be effected by him, but I was. I don't know why. I had my daughter with me. I was supposed to be a mom today, not some schoolgirl out with her crush. I needed to get a grip on myself before things got out of hand.

"I'll take care of that later," he leaned in and pecked my cheek.

"Ewww, gross!" Mara made a gagging sound from beside us causing Dev to chuckle.

"She doesn't miss anything, does she?" he leaned in next to me.

"Nope," I giggled as I leaned into his side.

Today was going to be fun. I'd dreamed of days like this for so long. I'd had them with Andy, and thought they were magical, but nothing compares to having the one you always pictured actually be there. Andy had filled the role that was always supposed to be Dev's. Being here like this had finally lifted the fog that had settled. Dev brought clarity, happiness, and most of all, love. I only hoped that Mara would fall for him as quickly as I had.

Chapter 14

We spent most of the afternoon walking around the outdoor exhibits, but as the air cooled and brought gray clouds with it, we moved indoors. The zoo was open year round, and because of the lovely winters that Chicago had, there were quite a few buildings with indoor exhibits. The monkeys were Mara's favorite, and Dev and I couldn't stop laughing as we watched her stand at the glass and mock them. She'd giggle whenever one would get close.

When we'd had our fill, Dev suggested we eat the dinner that we'd packed. It was getting late, and Mara had begun to get cranky. I knew the signs all too well. She was tired, and hungry, and probably should have had a nap.

When we stepped outside, a completely unexpected sight met us. The gray clouds that had been blowing in during the afternoon had opened up, and small snowflakes were falling. It wasn't uncommon to get snow this early in the year, but we had been totally unprepared.

"So much for our picnic," I mused as I stared up at Dev.

"Well, I kinda thought we might have to move it indoors. We can take it back to your place if you want," I smiled as Mara giggled.

"Yeah!" she clapped her hands from where she was perched on Dev's shoulders.

"We can talk," Dev murmured as he began leading us toward the car.

I nodded silently and followed him. The snow wasn't sticking. In fact, they were tiny little flakes, just barely visible. I knew that if the temperature kept dropping though it would stick around. Forget wishing for a white Christmas, we were going to get a white Thanksgiving.

"Mommy?" Mara yawned as Dev lifted her off his shoulders and set her in her seat. "Can we play in it?"

"I think that you might be too tired for that tonight. Maybe tomorrow?" I turned to face her from where I was sitting in the front.

"But…" she yawned again and Dev chuckled.

"She's stubborn like someone else I know," he mused.

I glared at him before turning back to her, "We'll have plenty of times to play in the snow. It'll be around a lot this winter."

"But, Mommmmy," Mara whined.

"Let's see if you can stay awake for the ride home, how's that?" I sighed as Dev cranked the car.

Our drive home was more eventful than we could have ever thought possible. Halfway there, we witnessed an accident. Someone was driving too fast, and when they went to brake, they slid through the intersection. Dev, being the cop that he is, pulled over to check on the drivers. Emergency workers hadn't appeared on the scene yet, so he waited by the accident.

By this time, the snow was falling heavier, and visibility sucked. We were still a good twenty-minute drive away from home, and Mara was barely awake.

"I'm hungry, Mommy," she mumbled as she fidgeted in her seat. I felt bad for her, but I really didn't know what to do. We were still waiting on Dev. He'd been directing traffic around the accident and was now helping the paramedics. I'd never seen him in action before except when he'd helped me. This was the dominating side of him. I knew it came from somewhere, but other than when he'd been bossing me around, I'd never seen it. The authority he possessed when he ordered onlookers to help, or move was nothing short of amazing. He wasn't prepared for the situation at all. No uniform, walkie-talkie, or badge. No blanket for the victim, or flares for the road. It was like everything he'd needed he didn't have. We'd taken my car that day, and I know that if we'd taken his, we'd have what he needed.

I watched as he shielded the snow from his eyes and came running to where we were waiting for him. He leaned in the door and huffed as he tried to catch his breath. "I can't leave yet," he sighed. "I have to fill out a report since I was first on the scene. I don't know how long that will take," his chin dropped before he glanced back at a now sleeping Mara. "I'm sorry. Why don't you take her home? I'll catch a ride with one of the other officers here and meet you at your place later."

"Ok," I murmured as I opened my door and moved around to the driver's side.

"I'm really sorry," he stood as I shivered in the cold. "I'll be as quick as I can. Be careful. It's really starting to get slick out here. I guess that polar vortex they were warning us about finally decided to show up."

"We can talk tomorrow," I mumbled as I looked away from him. The daylight was completely gone at this point, and only the street lamps and headlights illuminated the area. Flashers from two patrol cars blinked in the distance, and a fire truck had just pulled away.

"Sam," he tipped my chin up so he could see my eyes. "I meant what I said. I'll come by tonight."

"I know you did, but…" I looked away. "Mara's asleep, I'm hungry, and I know you're busy. We can talk in the morning, over breakfast maybe?"

"Ok," he relented. "I'll see you in the morning. Remember," he tipped his chin and kissed the tip of my nose, "be careful."

"I will," I rolled my eyes at him as I yanked open the driver's door and climbed in. I shivered as I adjusted the seat and mirrors so I could see. I checked on Mara one last time before shifting the car into drive and pulling out onto the street once again. I glanced in my rear view mirror to see Dev waving, as he got smaller and smaller. Soon he disappeared completely, and I was left in total darkness as I turned on the highway to head home.

The farther I drove, the worse the roads seemed to get. It wasn't that the snow was really deep or anything. In fact, that probably would have been better. An icy sheen coated the pavement and made you feel like you were driving on glass. I'd had a white-knuckle grip on the steering wheel for the last three miles and was silently cursing myself for not insisting that Dev drive us home. I had very little experience with this kind of weather and driving in it. I'd always walked or taken a cab. Now, if Chicago was going to be my permanent home, I guess I needed to change that.

"Mommy?" Mara's sleepy voice sounded from the backseat. "Are we there yet?"

"Almost, baby," I glanced back at her before turning back to the road. "Just a little farther."

We'd reached the outskirts of downtown at this point and as I began to get closer to downtown, I noticed that a few stoplights seemed to be out. "Great," I groaned under my breath. Could this day get any worse? If I'd known the answer to that question, I'd probably have never asked it.

Just as the light in front of me turned red, I began pumping my brakes. The car, however, wasn't stopping. Panic began to set in as we slid into the middle of the intersection. My rear end began to fish tail, and just as I'd righted myself, I looked up to see headlights shining brightly in my driver's side window. Before I could do anything, I heard it. Metal scraping, glass shattering, and a blood curdling scream. I wasn't sure if it was coming from me or my baby in the backseat. Time stopped as my brain fought to comprehend what had just happened.

"Miss?" I felt someone shaking my shoulder. "Miss? Oh god! There's a kid in the car," the voice was muffled and was getting quieter by the second. "Call 911," another voice called from somewhere in the distance.

"Dev?" my voice strained as I tried to open my eyes. "Help us," fell from my lips just as the darkness swallowed me up.

oooooooooo

Devlin

"What the fuck is taking so long," I grumbled as I turned to my partner who was now on the scene. "I need to get out of here."

"Relax," Jase chuckled. "She isn't going anywhere. I bet she's home right now keeping the bed warm for you."

I began pacing by the cruiser that waited for me to finish up at the scene. Jase was going to take me back to the station then give me a ride home.

"It's not like that," I growled. "She's not like that."

"Riiiight," Jase smirked. "You've been eyeing her since you got back to town. I know how it is with you when you set your sights on someone."

"All set boys. You can go now," the lead officer motioned for us to head back, and I shivered as I fought the cold. How had a day that started out so nice, turn so brutal so fast?

When we'd left this morning, I would have never thought that it would be snowing tonight. I guess I should have looked at the weather forecast better. I climbed in the cruiser, and smiled at Jase. "Let's get back to the station before my balls fall off from frostbite."

"No problem," he laughed. "What the hell were you doing out with only a fleece on today anyway?"

"I spent the day with Sam and my kid." I leaned back against the seat and closed my eyes on a sigh. "I'm tired, cold, and my feet are frozen... can we go now?"

"Touchy, touchy," he teased as he pulled out onto the road.

We drove at a fairly quick pace, considering the weather, but I was worried about my girls. Sam wasn't used to this shit weather dumped on us all of a sudden. I was berating myself for even letting her drive in it. I should have known better than to let her go, but seeing my daughter in the backseat begging to go home had caused my lack of good judgment.

"Fuccck another one?" Jase's voice brought me out of my thoughts. "Why the fuck can't the people that don't know how to drive in this stuff stay home?"

My head snapped up as realization began to sink in, "Shit!"

"Dude? What?" Jase turned on the lights and pulled over.

I shoved my door open before we even came to a complete stop. It couldn't be her. It couldn't, but as I ran up to the side of car, I couldn't deny it. Sam's car lay crumpled against the front end of a pickup truck. "No," I looked around at the wreckage.

"Come on," Jase tried to hold me back. "Take the car, I'll ride with someone else. They're at the hospital already. Chicago Memorial," he shoved the keys into my palm. "Go!" he turned me toward the car and then headed over to help the other officers on the scene.

Why the fuck hadn't I made her wait? This was all my fault. I kept chanting it over and over as I pulled out into traffic with the sirens on. The woman I loved was hurt along with my daughter who now might never know me. How the hell was I going to fix this?

Chapter 15

Devlin

When I reached the hospital, I pulled the cruiser into the fire lane, left the lights flashing, and rushed into the emergency room. A nurse was standing behind a desk looking more than annoyed at some guy who was hounding her.

"Sir, you need to have a seat or I'm going to have to call security," she pointed at a section of plastic chairs off to the side.

"I need answers now!" He pounded his fist on the counter and glowered at her.

"Sir..." she jumped back and her eyes flashed.

"You need to listen to her," I pointed at the nurse as I pulled my badge from my back pocket. "Go sit down!" I commanded as I pointed at the same set of chairs. I heard him grumble something under his breath, and if my brain wasn't spinning so fast, I might have pursued him. As it was, all I could think about was finding Sam and Mara. "Excuse me," I watched the young nurse. "I'm looking for two people that were brought in here tonight. A woman and a little girl? Samantha Connolly?"

"Let me check," the nurse smiled a thankful smile at me for dealing with her problem of the night and she clicked a few buttons on her computer screen. "Yes, Samantha Connolly is up in surgery right now, and Mara Ford is waiting on consent for treatment. You can go right down that hall and take two rights. She's in the third room."

"Thank you," I mumbled still in shock. I'd never asked Sam what name she'd given Mara. I never thought she'd give her mine. We hadn't discussed it, but apparently, she'd named our daughter after me.

"Officer?" the nurse called after me. "What do you need with Miss Ford?"

"I'm her father," I choked out. "I can give consent."

"You're Andrew Sommers?" the nurse's forehead crinkled in question.

My feet immediately stopped moving, and I almost tripped as I reached out and grabbed the wall. I slowly turned around, and I'm sure my face showed the panic I was feeling on the inside. "No, I'm her father," I stammered.

"The emergency contact information that was in Ms. Connolly's wallet listed a Mr. Andrew Sommers as the contact. We've called him, sir. He's on his way here from Las Vegas. I believe the last we heard he was on a plane and would get in around midnight."

"He's not her father," I uttered the words with as much force as I could. My baby was in there with some type of injury that needed treatment, and that guy who hadn't been here for them was gonna have a say in how she was treated.

"He's the one on the card. Do you have any proof that she's yours?" the nurse tried again, and I began walking in the direction of where she'd told me Mara was.

"No," I whispered as I sped up in search of her. When I reached her door, I slowly pushed it open. She was lying in the middle of a bed and covered in a pink blanket. The TV was on, but turned down very low and the lights were dim. Mara's eyes were closed, and I could see her chest rising and falling softly as she slept. A young woman was sitting in the corner dozing in a chair.

"They gave her something for the pain," she murmured when she looked up and saw me.

"What's wrong with her?" I approached the bed and noticed a bandage on her forehead.

"She's got a nice cut up there. I think a plastic surgeon is going to take a look at it in the morning. They want to make sure she doesn't get a scar on her face. She's got a broken arm, but it needs a pin inserted into the elbow. It's a spiral fracture, and it won't heal right without the pin. The doctors have to do surgery for that. They need consent. Who are you?"

She stood at this point and moved beside the bed. "I'm her father," I whispered as I watched her sleep. "Why are you here?"

"I'm the hospital's social worker. They called me to stay with her until someone came since she is so young. I was the one on call today," she reached up and clasped my shoulder. "They told me her father wasn't going to be in until much later."

"Andrew Sommers is not her father. He raised her, but he's not related to her," I growled with a mix of fear, sadness, and frustration. I couldn't believe that Sam had put him down as a contact. She'd been back here for over six months now. Why wouldn't she have added me?

"I'm gonna go now, unless you can't stay," the social worker peered up at me and smiled softly.

"Thank you," I nodded, "for staying with her."

"It's no problem," she said as she stepped out into the hall.

After the door closed softly, I dragged the chair she'd been sitting in over beside the bed. I sank down into it and reached for Mara's hand. After closing my hand around it softly, I let it all go. The fear that had taken up residence in me when I'd seen the car, the feeling that settled inside me when the nurse had told me Andy was coming, and all the worries that I'd been holding onto ever since I found out about her. She looked so fragile lying there, and as her father, I knew it was my job to protect her, no matter what. "I'm here now," I whispered as I leaned in and pressed a kiss to her forehead. 'I'm never gonna let anything happen to you ever again. I'll always protect you Mara. It's my job."

She stirred slightly causing me to pause in my confession, but soon settled back into sleep. "I love you." The tears I'd been fighting finally broke loose and began to trickle down my cheeks. I'd never been one to show my feelings. I'd learned a long time ago how to hide them. In my line of work, you couldn't feel. You had to lock things inside and find another way to let them out. I'd started out trying to hold it in, but later found that going to the gun range seemed to help. Recently, though, I'd been staying with Sam. Whenever I was around her things seemed to be easier. Life didn't hold as many doubts or letdowns, things were brighter, and seemed to be heading in a direction that was promising a future.

I wiped at my eyes as my shoulders slumped from exhaustion. It had been a tiring night, and the fear of what the morning held when Andy showed up was slowly taking its toll on me. I shifted in the chair and dropped my head to the bed. As my eyes drifted shut, I relaxed against the bed with my fingers still entwined with my daughter's. As bad as the circumstances were, I was finally getting to hold her. This was the closest I'd been since we met, and now that I knew what it felt like, I was never going to let go.

ooooooooo

As morning began to creep around me, I could hear hushed whispers. I couldn't make out exactly who was talking, but the ever-present giggle of my little girl was there in the mix. I could feel her leg moving under the covers where my head rested, and a quiet voice off in the distance. I didn't want to wake up, knowing where we were and who was going to be there today. The happiness in Mara's voice made the events of the night before seem distant. I wanted it to stay that way. I smiled with my eyes still closed as I released a yawn and rubbed at my eyes.

"He's waking up!" Her voice grew louder causing me to open my eyes.

What I saw in front of me sent my heart thundering in my chest, and the muscles there to squeeze tightly in a panic. There sitting perched on the bed right beside my daughter was the one person I had hoped to never meet.

"Hey!" she grinned. "Mr. Dev this is my Daddy," she pointed at him and smiled so big her face might spilt in two.

I glanced from her, up at him. He was tall and lean and looked like he might be a runner. His blonde hair was slightly shaggy, and his clothes were rumpled. The tie around his neck had been pulled loose, and part of his shirt untucked. He seemed older, and not anything like I expected.

"Nice to meet you," I held my hand out for him to shake as I reached across the bed. My voice held a warning that I'm sure he picked up on. His back had straightened, and his eyes watched me as if he was waiting for me to accuse him of something.

"I'm so glad you came," Mara looked up at him. "I knew you would. Mommy said we weren't going to see you anymore." Unbeknownst to her, she shoved that dagger that was in my chest just a little deeper every time she smiled at him and referred to him as her father.

"I'll always come when you need me," he ruffled her hair before moving to lean against the wall. By that time, a nurse had come in and pushed a syringe into Mara's IV.

"This will help relax her while we prep her for surgery to set the break and insert the pin. You're welcome to go grab some breakfast during the procedure. It's going to take a little while. Then we'll be moving her upstairs to share a room with her mother," the nurse was pulling the side rails up at this point and motioning for help from more of the staff. As Mara was wheeled out of the room, I glared and the man that was threatening my family.

"I need to talk to you," I scowled as I pointed at him. He nodded as he followed me out of the room. We paused in the waiting area, and I pointed at the door, "You can go now."

"I'm not leaving until Samantha asks me to," he crossed his arms over his chest.

"I'm Mara's father, not you!" I pointed at my chest as I felt it tighten.

"Biologically," he sneered. "I raised her. I was the one who held her when she was born. I went to all of Samantha's appointments. I got up at night when she cried. I took care of her when she was sick, bandaged scraped knees, held her hand on the first day of pre-school... me! Not you!" He pounded his fist against his chest. "You may have donated the sperm, but you are not her father."

I could feel the anger simmering just below the surface. I was fighting very hard against every instinct I had. My brain was warring between taking this douche outside and pounding his face in or calming the fuck down and being there for my daughter. The fact that she'd introduced him to me as her 'daddy' had almost made me tell her who I was right there. I knew that Sam wanted to be the one to tell her, though and I couldn't take that away from her. I couldn't take what was already a scary event and turn it into something she wouldn't understand.

"You may have been there, but I didn't miss those by choice," I growled. "I didn't know about her," I began pacing the waiting room. "Sam couldn't tell me," I huffed under my breath. "I tried..." I swallowed as my eyes squeezed shut. "I tried to find her. I loved her, I still do," I darted my eyes in his direction and I'm sure he could see the pain that was spread across my face. "Did she tell you? Do you know what happened with us? Did she tell you how much she loved me? Wanted me? Begged me to come with her?" I moved and stood in front of him. "I bet all those nights her body was in your bed, her heart and mind were in mine," I nodded as I swallowed. "I bet she secretly wished that you were me, every time your hands touched her, she felt me. Every time she snuggled up to you, she was with me. Every time she looked at that little girl in there, she saw me. I know this because that little girl," I pointed in the direction that they had rolled Mara. "She looks just like me!"

He stood there stunned as his face grew redder and redder, "You don't know shit about Samantha and I, or Mara for that matter," he hissed. "Not once did she mention you in the four years we were together."

"She couldn't, don't you get that?" I shook my head as a self-deprecating laugh slipped out. "It was against the rules. She was protecting herself, but now…" I chuckled. "She doesn't need to be protected anymore and she's here with me and we don't need you."

"But you do," he chuckled. "You needed me so she could get treated. You see," he shrugged, "you're not on the list."

"Not for long," I growled as I turned toward the elevators.

"Where are you going?" he chased after me.

"To see my girlfriend and sort this shit out," I turned on him. "You will be leaving today. You won't be coming back, and Mara is MY daughter," I pushed the 'close door' button as soon as I slipped through the doors.

Sam was up on the fourth floor and should be awake by now. She'd had to have her spleen removed the night before, but everything had gone well. Now, I was going to have to drop this bomb on her. She needed to tell this character that he was not wanted or needed, and that he needed to go back to fucking Vegas.

Chapter 16

Samantha

Pain… that was all I could feel. My side had a shooting pain in it every time I tried to shift my body. I couldn't really remember what had caused it. The night before was fuzzy at best, but pieces were slowly coming back. Lights, scraping metal, ice, crying… My eyes flew open, and I tried to sit up only to be held down by tubes and blankets. I groaned as I let my eyes adjust to the light.

"Easy," Dev's voice was barely a whisper.

"What happened?" I moistened my lips and blinked a few times.

"You were in an accident. You're okay," he brushed a few strands of hair off my forehead.

"Mara?" I began to panic.

"She's okay, too," he swallowed.

"Where is she?" I tried to lift my head, but the throbbing in it caused me to wince and give up.

"She broke her arm," he sighed. "The doctors have to put a pin in the elbow. They're working on it right now," he lifted my hand and threaded his fingers between mine. "I need to tell you something and you need to promise me that you're gonna listen and relax."

I tried to nod, but my head was throbbing so bad that I stopped, "Okay."

"When I got here last night," he looked away for a minute, "they had her downstairs. The nurse said they needed consent, but you were in surgery so they got the contact info from your wallet."

I knew what was coming next. He didn't need to say anymore. The look on his face said it all. He lifted my hand to his lips and kissed the back of it as he squeezed it. "Baby…"

"I know," I swallowed. "He's here, isn't he?"

Dev slowly nodded as the door to my room opened. The figure standing there was one I hadn't seen in months. He looked worn and tired. His clothes were a mess, and he was sporting what looked like a two-day-old beard.

"Hi," he murmured as he shuffled in the room.

"Andy," I whispered. "What are you doing here?"

"They called me about Mara. How are you?" He sank down in the chair that was across the room.

"I've been better," I groaned as I shifted to look in his direction. "We need to talk." I looked over at Dev, "Can you get me some water?"

His head bobbed slowly as he stood, grabbed the pitcher off the counter, and exited the room. "You need to leave," I peered over at Andy as Dev left the room.

"What?" he gasped.

"You need to leave," I tried again with a little more conviction in my voice.

"I'm not leaving until I know you're ok," he crossed his foot over his knee. "If you didn't want me here, you wouldn't have left me on your list of contacts. I think deep down inside you knew you'd need me."

My eyes flashed as I watched his. Was he for real? I had totally forgotten about the emergency contact info. I hadn't even thought about changing it. I was dating a police officer. I didn't think I'd have to worry about this stuff now.

"We're not together. We're not going to be together. Nothing's changed. I love him," I pointed to where Dev was now standing in the doorway. "He loves me and Mara. You can leave."

"You heard her," Dev's voice was ominous. I could see the ticking in his jaw and knew that he and Andy must have had words. The only time Dev let his anger show was when it was something to do with me. He was jealous, and as much as that flattered me, I just wanted Andy to go. I didn't want to be with him. Dev knew this.

"Please?" I turned my head to stare at Andy. "If you care about me at all, you'll leave."

"I'll be back tomorrow so we can talk... alone," he eyed Dev before sauntering over to the door. He paused a moment before looking back at me, "Nothing's changed for me either, Samantha. I still love you, and I love our little girl. I plan on taking you both back to Vegas with me. You'll see; it's the right thing to do." He turned back around and slipped through the door leaving me speechless.

I glanced up to see Dev glowering at Andy's retreating form. "I'm not going with him and neither is Mara. Don't worry; I want to be with you," I reached for his hand and waited for him to acknowledge me. "Do you hear what I'm saying? I want you, not him."

Dev sighed and sank down onto the edge of the bed, "You have to tell her—today. She introduced me to her 'daddy' this morning. I can't keep acting like she's not mine." His eyes held pain, and he was almost begging me. "The doctors are going to let her go home today. They're bringing her up here after her surgery. I want to take her with me. Your mom said she'd come get her, but I want to take her with me. Please tell me you're ok with that?"

"She's not going to understand, and she'll probably be mad when I tell her. I don't know if she'll go willingly," I mumbled. "We can see how things go and then decide."

"I can live with that," Dev leaned over and pressed a kiss to my forehead. "You need to rest. I'm not going anywhere until you're better. So, close your eyes and get some rest. I'll wake you as soon as Mara's out of surgery. Okay?"

I shifted and winced in the bed before trying to find a comfortable position. "Can you ask the nurse for something for the pain? I can't sleep like this," I grimaced.

"Sure thing," he smiled at me as he stood and leaned out the door.

Within seconds, a nurse was coming in and squeezing something into one of the plastic tubes attached to me. She smiled softly at Dev as she left. I knew that look. I saw him get them all the time. Hell, I wore that smile when I looked at him. As thoughts of a future with him, and finally being able to tell my daughter about him settled into my brain, I began to drift off. The quiet beeping of the machines lulled me into a deep drug- filled sleep.

ooooooooo

"Mommy?" I could hear the voice, but my eyes didn't open as fast as I'd have liked. "Mommy?" she nudged me on the shoulder.

"Mommy's tired," Dev whispered. "Let's let her sleep. You can sit here with me. Wanna read a story?"

When she agreed, I let myself be dragged back into a deep sleep.

A few hours later, I'm not sure how long; I began to wake again. I turned my head just in time to see Dev seated in a rocking chair by the window. Mara was curled in his lap, her arm wrapped in a bright pink cast, and her head resting on his chest. One arm was holding her against his chest while the other softly brushed her hair across her forehead. He was murmuring something so quietly I couldn't make it out, but the scene before me made my chest tighten. I'd waited years for this.

Mara stirred slightly as her eyes blinked. "Mommy!" she cheered as she scrambled to climb out of his lap. Her face twisted in pain and she whimpered.

"Easy there," Dev soothed. "You're arm's gonna be sore for a while."

"It hurts," she whined. "Make it stop."

"We need to get your medicine from the store," he grimaced. He then directed his gaze at me, "She wanted to wait until she got to see you before leaving."

"Come here, baby," I patted a spot beside me. "I need to talk to you."

Mara shuffled over to the bed, and Dev helped her climb up. She was going to have to learn to do things with one arm, but I had a feeling it wouldn't take her long to master it. Kids were always bouncing back from things like this.

"Where's Daddy?" She watched me and tears began to gather in her eyes. "You made him leave, didn't you?" she scowled.

"Mara," I took a deep breath. "I need to tell you something, and I want you to listen carefully, ok?" She nodded slowly as her forehead creased. "You know how we talked about families back when we lived in Nevada. You wanted to know why Mommy and Daddy weren't married." I waited as she slowly nodded in understanding. "I told you that all families were different... that some only had a mommy and others only had a daddy?"

"You said that mommies and daddies don't make a family, love does," she lifted her hand and began nibbling on her index finger.

"And I said that sometimes when a mommy or a daddy can't take care of the baby that someone else helps out?" I kept watching her hoping that she'd forgive me one day for doing this to her.

"Uh huh," her eyes dropped to her lap before she looked back up at me. A single tear trickled down her cheek before she looked over at Dev and then back at me.

"Andy's not your daddy, baby," I reached up and tucked a piece of hair behind her ear as the tears in her eyes spilled out onto her cheeks. "Dev's your daddy," I nodded to where he was now leaning forward from the chair by the bed. Mara sat unmoving as her little brain tried to process the bomb I'd just dropped on her.

She turned to look at Dev, tears streaming down her face as her voice came out in choked sobs. "Didn't you want me?"

"Oh sweetheart, I didn't know about you," he opened his arms to her as she shuffled toward him, and finally fell into his arms. "I could never not want you. I love you."

Mara sniffled as she used her good hand to wipe the tears from her eyes. "Are we gonna live with you now?"

"I hope so... one day," Dev pressed a kiss to the top of her head. My mouth dried instantly as I sucked in a breath. I'd dreamed, hoped, and prayed for this. I'd never thought it would actually happen though. I'd convinced myself that the man I'd met all those years ago was a figment of my imagination.

When we reconnected, he'd changed. He'd gone from the sweet boy I knew in high school, to a dominating man who knew exactly what he wanted in life. When I had to leave him four years ago, I'd hoped that one day we would get back what we had, but I never thought it would be a reality. Now, as I watched him with our daughter, I realized that all the good I'd seen over the years is still there. Beneath the strong, tough exterior was a gentle, loving father.

"Mara," I hated to break the moment, but I wanted to make sure she was ok with going home with Dev or if I needed to call my mother. She looked up at me, but kept her iron grip on him. "I have to stay here tonight," I winced. The pain meds were wearing off, but I'd refused the meds when I woke up because I knew I needed a clear head for this discussion. "Would you like Dev to stay with you tonight or do you want me to call Grandma to take you home with her? If Dev takes you home, you can sleep in your own bed and be comfortable."

She looked from me to him several times before she put her head on his chest. Without looking up, she mumbled, "Can I call you Daddy?"

I watched the strong man who I'd never seen cry, shed tears for the second time in less than twelve hours. His shoulders shook as he fought to hold himself together. "Yes baby, you can call me Daddy."

She turned her head as she nuzzled deeper into his embrace before looking back at me, "I wanna stay with Daddy."

I smiled as I too began to cry. My hand flew to my mouth as I tried to control myself. It hurt when I breathed deeply, and my emotions had taken about all they could stand. "My keys are in my purse, wherever that is."

I watched Dev whisper something into her ear before she climbed out of his arms and took a seat in one of the chairs by the window. He slowly rose and stood beside the bed. He leaned down, and pressed a kiss against my forehead as he uttered, "Thank you. I promise," he swallowed, "I'll never hurt her. I'll always be here… for both of you."

"I know," I mumbled as my eyes connected with his. "I'll deal with Andy. You take our daughter home, and let her get some rest."

"I'll come back tomorrow morning," he whispered. "You get some rest, too."

He turned, leaned down, and opened his arms once again. Mara ran to him this time and giggled when he lifted her into the air. "Tell Mommy you'll see her in the morning," he kissed her cheek.

"Bye, Mommy," Mara cooed as she leaned her head down on his shoulder and wrapped her arms around his neck. It was awkward with the cast, but neither one seemed to mind.

As I shifted once again, I watched two of the most important people in my life slip out the door leaving me in silence. I knew Andy wasn't going to accept my decision, but he wasn't Mara's father. He had done a great job helping me and Mara loved him, but he could never replace Dev. Dev had always been there—in the back of mind. He'd written his name on my heart when we were seventeen. Now that we were back together, he'd branded it.

Chapter 17

When I awoke the next morning, the reality that I'd been dreading hit me full force right in the face. Sitting in a chair in the corner, sipping his coffee, was Andy. He placed the paper cup on the windowsill and smiled at me, "Good morning."

"Morning," I groaned.

"How are you feeling?" He stood and wiped his palms down the front of his jeans.

"Like I got hit by a truck," I grumbled as I reached to prop the bed up. Andy stood there watching as I struggled to sit up and swing my legs over the edge of the bed. I'd been given permission the night before to get out of bed, and now that nature was calling, I was fighting against the pain. "Don't help me or anything," I rolled my eyes and my muscles shook as I tried to stand.

Andy shook his head and muttered, "Too damn independent," as he wrapped an arm around my back and guided me into the bathroom.

"You can go now," I grumbled as I pulled away from him.

"Samantha," he sighed as he let his head drop back and stared at the ceiling.

"What?" I narrowed my eyes on him. "I want privacy."

"We slept together for almost four years; you're being ridiculous," he shook his head at me.

"Maybe," I reached for the door and began closing it, "but I want you out," I shut it in his face.

"You have to talk to me," he yelled through the door. "I'm not going away until you do."

After relieving myself and washing my hands, I stood there staring in the mirror at my reflection. I had a bruise on my neck where my seatbelt had held me in. My eyes were puffy, and I had burn marks on my arms from the air bag. I lifted the gown I was wearing to see a bandage on my side where the doctors had removed my spleen. The gauze over the incision was surrounded by bruises. I was a mess. There was no way I was going to be going back to work anytime soon.

Work. Just thinking about it put me in panic mode. Who was taking care of the bar? Was it even open? Did they know what had happened to me? Dev hadn't mentioned it, and with the weather and the accident, I wasn't sure what was going on. My thoughts had been so consumed with Mara, Dev, and Andy that The Rusty Nail had taken a backseat in my thoughts.

I released a deep breath and cringed. I ached, and I'd told the nurse I didn't want the pain meds today. They'd told me this morning that if the doctor agreed, I could go home tomorrow, but I'd have to rest. No work or heavy lifting for at least a week.

I turned and pushed the door open just as Andy was lifting his hand to knock on it. "Thought you might have fallen in or something," he chuckled.

I glared at him as I refused his help and shuffled over to the bed. After climbing in and tugging the covers up, I took a deep breath to prepare myself to deal with him. "You need to go back to Vegas."

"I told you I will. I'm waiting for you to be healed enough to travel. You and Mara are coming with me. I took time off to stay until you can travel," he crossed his arms over his chest and leaned against the wall, challenging me.

"I'm going to make this as clear as I can. I'm not going with you, and neither is Mara. I live here now. Mara has friends, her grandmother, and school. More importantly, she has her father," I leaned back on the pillows behind me and squeezed my eyes shut against the pain.

"About that," Andy shifted, and I heard his footsteps right before I felt the bed dip. "He can't give you what I can."

"And what's that," I kept my eyes closed and waited.

"Stability," he sighed. "I can be there... for whatever you need. I'm not going to just disappear and leave you. Mara needs a father she can count on, one that can be there for all the important moments in her life. He can't."

My eyes opened, and I bit down on the inside of my cheek as his words sunk in. "That's not his fault," I argued. I understood what Andy was saying. I knew that Dev's job prevented him from being there all the time, but I also knew that I loved him and he loved both Mara and me. He would do everything in his power to be there for us, and if he couldn't, it wouldn't be from lack of trying.

I had a feeling that Andy just wanted to win whatever battle he thought this was. He hadn't mentioned Mara at all today except for talking about her going back to Vegas with him. For all I knew, he didn't even know that Mara had gone home with Dev. "I told her," I whispered and watched his back stiffen. I didn't want to be cruel about any of this, but Andy just wasn't getting it. "Yesterday... I told her Dev was her father."

"And how did that go?" he growled.

"She was confused at first, but then happy. I think she always knew something was different between us. She probably didn't even know that she knew it, but children are very perceptive."

"I'll bet he loooooved that," Andy huffed. "Where is he anyway? If he loves you so much, why isn't he here? Isn't he man enough to talk to me himself?"

"He was taking care of his daughter, you jackass," Dev's voice came in a low growl as he leaned against the doorjamb.

Andy rose from the bed and turned to face Dev. He shoved his hands in the pockets of his jeans and puffed his chest out. "You lost your chance at this family when you walked away from her. Why don't you go back to wherever you were and leave us alone."

"Andy!" I gasped. My eyes welled with tears as I watched Dev. I knew the truth. He loved me. He loved Mara, and I was not going to let Andy try to beat him into an emotional submission.

"I think I'll stay," Dev's lips curved up on one side. "I'll leave when she asks me to," he pointed at me as he pushed off the jamb and strutted over to the bed. His eyes stared daggers into Andy as he leaned over and brushed his lips across mine. It was a soft sweet kiss, but soon turned into something that shouldn't have been on display.

When I didn't pull away, he pressed his mouth more firmly to mine, and cupped my jaw. I opened up to him letting him in to mark me. His tongue ran along my bottom lip as his teeth took small nips. I sighed as I let him sink further into my mouth, devouring me more by the minute. He groaned as I broke the kiss and smiled at him. His eyes had darkened, and he shifted on his feet trying to hide what I'd just done to him. "She's not interested in you anymore," Dev's voice held amusement as he pecked my forehead before standing back up and turning to glare at Andy.

"I'm sorry," I watched the emotions pass over his face before he finally began to accept the inevitable. "I didn't want to hurt you, but I…" I swallowed and watched as his head slowly shook.

He held up a hand to silence me as his gaze dropped to the floor, "I get it. I love you, but I guess it's not enough. I hope you're happy with him."

"I am very happy," I smiled as I turned to look up at Dev.

"Thank you," Dev nodded at Andy, "for taking care of my girls. I really mean that."

Andy's head bobbed slowly as he turned away from us and moved toward to the door. He paused for a moment with his hand on the knob. "Take care of them," he whispered before opening to door and slipping into the hallway. I knew by the sound of his voice that he'd finally let me go. He was moving on and accepting the fact that I was happy— I hoped.

ooooooooo

Devlin

"Mara, you ready yet?" I called as I shuffled the mail around on the kitchen table. I'd tossed Sam's keys down when I'd come home earlier in the morning. Georgia, Mara's grandmother,

~ 208 ~

had come to stay with her while I went to the hospital, but now we needed to go back and pick up Sam. She'd finally convinced that dick, Andy, to leave, and now they were letting her come home. It'd been three days, and it was the longest three days of my life. I'd spent them taking care of my daughter, and even though I'd never seen myself as a dad, I was quickly learning the ropes.

"In a minute," Mara's voice rang out from somewhere down the hall.

"We need to go so we can bring Mommy home," I called back as I sighed in relief when my fingertips brushed across the key ring under the mail. When Mara emerged, it took everything in me not to laugh. She stood there in a pair of pink shorts, a bright blue sweatshirt that looked to be two sizes too big, and a pair of rain boots.

"I'm done," she lifted her arms before letting them drop to her sides in a dramatic sigh.

"It's twenty degrees outside, baby. You can't wear shorts," I chuckled.

"But I wanna," she whined as her lip popped out in a pout.

"Would Mommy let you wear shorts in the snow?" I tried to reason with her, and the fact that she was three didn't even register in my mind.

"Uh huh," she nodded as she tried to cross her arms. The cast on her right one made it difficult though.

Being a dad was still so new that I wasn't really sure how to deal with this situation, so rather than argue with her, I tried to compromise. I twisted my mouth in concentration before walking over to the coat rack. I'd left a winter coat here when I came to stay the night with her, and I was now wearing my police coat. "How about you keep this warm for me?" I shrugged out of the heavy police jacket as I wrapped it around her tiny shoulders. It dwarfed her, coming all the way down to her knees and past her fingertips.

"It's too big," she giggled as she lifted her arms.

"We can fix that," I knelt down in front of her and gently pushed the sleeves up to expose her hands. I zipped up the front so her legs were covered and then stepped back. "There," I grinned at her.

"I look like you, Daddy," she giggled.

"That you do, baby. Keep that warm for me, ok?" I ruffled her hair before grabbing my other coat and slipping it on. "Let's go get Mommy.

She's waiting on us," I reached for her tiny hand as I stuffed my wallet and badge in my pocket and led her from the condo. I could handle this dad stuff. It wasn't as hard as my buddies at the station had made it out to be.

ooooooooo

Samantha

The doctors had cleared me to go home, and as I sat on the edge of my bed waiting for Dev, my mind swarmed with 'what ifs'. I couldn't help but wonder how things were going back at my condo. Mara was a good kid, but with the snow and a broken arm, I was sure she was driving him nuts.

I watched out the window as the snow continued to fall. It'd been coming down nonstop since the night of the accident. I wondered how Mara would be in the snow. Would she like it as I had as a child? She'd never seen snow before except in the movies we watched. Vegas didn't get snow. Heck, it was warm enough sometimes that you could swim this time of year.

"Mommy!" Mara squealed as she burst through the door causing me to jump from my musings.

"Hey, baby," I smiled at her and fought to hold back a laugh when I saw how she was dressed. Her blonde hair was pulled in a

~ 211 ~

messy ponytail that was crooked, and other than Dev's coat, which was pretty much covering her, all you could see were the rain boots peeking out of the bottom.

"Don't ask," Dev muttered as he released a deep breath. "She wanted to dress herself."

"You can tell her no, you know," I rolled my eyes and smirked at him. "She doesn't always have to get what she wants."

"I missed three years of spoiling her," he ran his hand through his damp hair. The snow that had been stuck there was melting causing tiny water droplets to appear. "I'm not telling her 'no' for a long time."

"So I get to be the bad guy?" I grinned. "Thanks," I giggled as I gripped my side in pain. "Don't make me laugh. It hurts too much," I chastised him.

"Sorry," he winked as he moved to sit beside me. He leaned closer to my ear and whispered, "I know I can't let her do whatever she wants, but I don't want to tell her no on the small stuff. She's had a rough couple of days, too."

"I get it, I do, but you do have to learn to be firm," I smiled at him before turning back to watch our daughter. She was jumping across the room, using the floor tiles to play some made up game that only she knew the rules.

"Can we go now?" she grinned up at us.

"Yep," I pushed myself to a standing position. I grimaced as I tried to put my coat on, and Dev helped me.

"Good," Mara nodded. "I need my hair fixed the right way, and Daddy can't do it like you do."

"Oh really?" Dev teased. "Maybe Mommy can teach me," he winked as a laugh escaped before helping me into the wheelchair that had just been rolled into the room.

"I think we can arrange that," I lowered myself into the seat and turned to face Mara, "You want to ride on my lap down to the car?"

Mara's little head bobbed furiously before she scurried over and attempted to climb into my lap. Dev reached for her so she wouldn't hurt me and helped her settle into my arms before telling the nurse he'd take it from there.

When we left the hospital that day, I couldn't help but think that we'd rounded a corner. Something had changed in all of us. A future was being forged, and the obstacles that lay ahead seemed more like speed bumps than mountains. I knew we still had a long way to go before we'd be the happy family that I envisioned, but we were heading in the right direction. We'd get there... soon... I hoped.

Chapter 18

"So you're sure everything is fine? You don't need me to stop by today?" I leaned back on my couch with the phone pressed to my ear.

"You concentrate on getting better. We've got everything under control here," Tiff's voice was muffled as I heard her turn away from the phone and yell at someone to be more careful.

"You sure about that?" I laughed and clutched my side where it still ached.

"We're fine," she sighed. "It's just the new girl you hired is having a hard time behind the bar. She's broken a few glasses. She thinks that since she was hired as a waitress, she would only be doing that. I've tried to tell her that we all do everything here. Mason is helping though. You should consider having him tend bar as well as bounce. He's pretty good back here," she giggled.

"Well, I should be back on Monday. The doctors gave me the all clear for next week," I shifted and scratched lightly at my bandage. The stitches itched, and I was trying with all my might not to touch them.

"Take your time, girl; you didn't hire me for nothing," she chirped right before disconnecting the call.

"Goodbye to you, too," I muttered as I shook my head.

"Something wrong?" Dev rounded the couch and sat down before pulling my feet into his lap.

"No, I'm just not used to this," I mumbled as I leaned back and closed my eyes. I couldn't help the moan that slipped out when I felt his thumbs press into the soles of my feet. "That feels soooo good."

"Not used to what?" He totally ignored my last statement as his fingers danced up my ankles and began to work the knots out of my calves.

"Having people do all this for me. I've always— oh god!" I groaned.

"Do what?" his voice was light as he continued to torture me. I knew he was fighting to keep things from going further. We hadn't been together in over a week and weren't supposed to be for another three days. If he wanted me half as much as I wanted him, he was showing great restraint.

"Take care of me," I tossed my hand in the air. "I've always taken care of myself. I've never wanted to rely on anyone."

"Well," he shifted so he was closer to my head "I plan on taking care of both of you. No more worrying about anything. You and Mara," he leaned in a pressed a kiss to my forehead, "you're my top priority."

"What about work?" I mumbled. I knew that with his job we never knew what the next day held. He could be sent out on assignment, and there was nothing I could do about it. "What if you have to go under again?"

Dev sighed as he leaned back on the couch and let his head drop back. He pinched the bridge of his nose as his head tipped toward the ceiling. "That's who I am, Sam. I can't change that, but I'm damn well gonna do what I can when I'm here. There are cops that are married and have families. It's not something that I ever thought about before. I love you," he turned his head to the side and stared at me. "I wanna be here… for you… for Mara. I wanna take care of you, if you'll let me."

"I know you do. I just," I swallowed hard and looked away before mumbling, "What if you get sent away for a long time again? What if something happens? How would I ever know about it?" I knew all these fears that I was laying out for him were real. They could very well happen, and there wasn't anything I could do.

"What do you want me to do? Quit?" His face twisted as he watched me.

"I would never ask you to do that, but I'm scared," my voice trembled as the tears rose to the surface. We'd never really talked about this, but Dev wanted to define whatever we were, and he wanted to do it now.

"Scared of what?" he sat up and ran his palm up my thigh.

"Losing you," I bit my lip and wiped at my eyes. "I can't let you in again only to have you ripped away. What happens when you go back under and Mara asks me when you're coming back? What do I tell her?"

"That'll always be a chance, but right now... things are good. All but one of the cases I've worked is closed, and the open one... Jase is running point. I'm not going to lie to you. It could come to me leaving again, but not for years at a time. I'm not missing anymore of her childhood," he pointed toward the hallway where Mara was playing in her room. "Are we good?"

I shrugged, "As good as it's going to get today."

"Sam," he sighed.

"No, really. I'm fine. I'm just feeling bad over the fact that I'm stuck here and everyone seems to have everything under control. I guess I'm just a little stir crazy," I offered a weak smile.

"Well, Thanksgiving is next week. I told your mom we'd cook, and she could come here to eat. You'll be back to normal by then, and I think I have an idea of what we can do to pep you up," His eyes twinkled with mischief as he grinned at me.

"You're so bad," I rolled my eyes as I swatted at his arm.

"You love it," he snickered.

"Down boy," laughed and gripped my side that still ached. "Ow!" I groaned.

oooooooooo

When Monday rolled around, I was itching to get out of the condo. My mother had stopped by that morning to take Mara to pre-school. They were having some kind of grandparent

~ 218 ~

luncheon that week for Thanksgiving, and Mara hadn't stopped talking about it all weekend. My mother was all smiles as they disappeared out into the snow.

The weather hadn't gotten any worse, but it was still freezing cold, and we had about eight inches of fluffy white mess on the ground. I was over it. I missed the warm fall weather that Vegas had. The only perk to living here was the man sitting at the table stuffing cereal into his mouth.

"So I'll see you tonight?" I was tugging on a hat and gloves as I turned to face Dev.

"I gotta work the late shift tonight. I can come by here after, if you want me too, but I don't know what time that'll be," he mumbled as he scanned the paper in front of him. "They want extra help this week with the holidays and all. It brings out the crazies."

I nodded as I chewed the inside of my mouth, "Ok."

"Sam," Dev blew out a breath. "Don't do that."

"Do what?" I turned and glared at him.

"I've been staying here the last nine days. I've been with you more than I've been at work. They've given me all the time off that I've asked for, even though it's been busy. Jase has run interference at the station with the Captain. What more do you want from me?"

"It's nothing," I murmured. "I just miss you when you're gone. I've gotten used to having you here, and well, tonight, you know," I glanced away as my cheeks reddened.

I heard the chair scrape against the floor as he shoved back from the table. His bare feet padded over to stand behind me. "I know exactly what today is," he murmured in my ear. "I've been counting down the hours until this day arrived," his nose skimmed up the column of my neck before he nipped my ear. "I'll do what I can to get home before it's too late, but sometimes things happen that I can't control," he pecked my cheek before stepping away from me.

The loss of heat from him caused me to shudder, "You're so mean."

Within seconds, he stormed back up to me, spun me around, and pressed me into the wall behind us, "You have no idea how mean I can really be." His eyes darkened as he pressed his hips firmly to mine. The flannel lounge pants he was wearing did nothing to hide his excitement. It had been eleven days now, and it was more than obvious that he needed me as much as I needed him. His head moved closer as his eyes darted between my lips and my eyes. "I can tease and taunt you so much that you won't even remember your own name," he leaned next to my ear. "We have a third person living here with us though, so we have to figure out a way to keep you quiet," he mumbled.

"I c– c– can b– be quiet," I stammered.

"Riiiiight," he teased as one hand moved from where it was holding my shoulder and drifted between my legs. "Shit, babe," he growled. "You need to go to work," he shoved away from me and just as I was beginning to protest, my phone chimed.

I swallowed and tried to calm myself as I pulled it out of my coat pocket and looked at the caller ID... Tiff. "What's up?" I tried to sound normal.

"You coming in today?" she giggled. "You're never late."

"I'm on my way out the door right now," I rolled my eyes as I heard Dev snicker in the background. Oh, he was so going down for this. I was going to get him back and make him pay for winding me up so tight.

"Well, hurry up. The liquor order is coming in in an hour, and I want you here so we can go over drinks for the holiday menu," she clicked off the line. Tiff had a bad habit of hanging up on me lately. It was as if she knew when the conversation was over and didn't want to delay the disconnection.

"Crazy woman," I muttered as I scowled at Dev. He was laughing at the table when I shoved my phone back in my pocket. I turned to face him as I slowly shook my head, "It's on big boy. You and me— this isn't over. You've stuck your hand in a hornets nest, and I'm one angry hornet."

"Bring it, babe," he chided just as I closed the door to my condo.

We needed to fix this living situation. Dev living upstairs was dumb. My face almost split in two as the idea of living together popped into my brain. We'd never discussed it, but it made sense that he move into my place. He practically lived there already anyway. I couldn't remember the last time he's stayed at his apartment instead of mine.

When I got downstairs, the idea had grown into a plan. I'd ask him tomorrow. The bar was closed for the remainder of the week for the holiday. I didn't believe that my employees should have to work on the holidays, so I was just planning to stay closed. We'd have plenty of time to move his things if he agreed to it. Just because he had to work didn't mean that I couldn't do this for him. Yep, tomorrow would be moving day.

I smiled at my revelation as I climbed into the blue Trailblazer. Dev had insisted that I start driving one of his vehicles since my car had been totaled. The Trailblazer had been in a storage locker during the summer because it was his winter car. He swapped out the motorcycle when the weather changed. As I settled into the seat, and adjusted the mirrors, I took a deep breath. It smelled like him, and I couldn't help but feel giddy like a young girl with her first crush.

It wasn't that I'd never done something like this; it was more the fact that it meant something this time. These were simple things that I'd never had. The little moments that most people take for granted. I'd hidden my heart so far away for so long that I hadn't really let myself feel things. Things like borrowing a sweatshirt, having breakfast together, falling asleep watching a movie— I'd had those with Andy, but it didn't feel the same.

With Andy, I was pretending to be someone else. My body was there, but my heart was tucked away because I knew that it wasn't permanent. Now, I was back, and I was Sam. I wasn't hiding myself from anyone. I was the *me* that I was meant to be, and Dev... he wanted that *me*. He wanted the *us* that I'd dreamed about for so long, and I was going to make sure we got it.

Chapter 19

The bar was crazy tonight. I think every person in Chicago decided to come out and see the band we'd booked. Tiff and I handled the bar once again. Courtney, the new girl, was still too green to be bartending, and I needed Mason at the door. I really was going to have to reevaluate the situation. Chris's band was doing better, and if I didn't watch it, he was going to end up leaving me short-staffed. I was happy for him, but with the way things had been going lately it looked like I was going to be doing more of what I was tonight and less managing.

"Holy crap, I'm tired!" I groaned as I tugged my tee from my jeans. "I think we served half the city tonight."

"That's a good thing," Tiff smirked from beside me as she took the garnish tray and began emptying it. "With the bar closed the rest of the week, this will give us the funds we all need to survive until Monday."

"I know you need the money, but aren't happy to have holidays off?" I began wiping down tables as she stocked the beer cooler.

"Yeah, I like having the time off. I just wish I had someone to spend it with," Tiff muttered.

"What? I thought you and Jase…" I stopped mid-sentence when she held her hand up. "Tiff?"

"That's not going to happen," she sighed as she slumped against the counter behind her.

"What? Why? I thought things were moving along for you two." I tossed my rag onto the bar and sat down on a stool. "Talk to me."

"Something happened," she shook her head and continued to stare at the ground. "We were doing ok, I guess, if you could call it that. I mean— I don't know if we really were a 'we'," she looked up at me and I saw a look that I'd never seen before from Tiff. She looked genuinely hurt. "He's got demons; that's for sure. We've been messing around for a couple of weeks. It was ok, I mean, it was for fun, no strings," she shrugged and then leaned forward to rest her elbows on the bar. "He never promised me anything, and I didn't ask. It was fun, ya know?" she shrugged.

"You really like him, don't you?" I reached across the bar and covered her hand with mine.

"I thought I did," her eyes met mine and filled with tears. "I can't get close enough to really figure it out. Every time I try to get him to let me, he shut down. It's as if he has this wall up, and he's not going to let anyone in. You can see it in his face when we're together. His expressions, they show love, or at least I think they do, but when I try to get him to open up, the bricks fly into place and he shuts down. For the life of me, I can't get through."

"Have you talked to him about this? Dev had a wall up when we reconnected. He didn't let me in and was always pulling away," I soothed as I watched a tear slip down her cheek.

"Dev was undercover. He had to hide stuff from you. "I'm not hiding anything from Jase."

"You might not be, but he has things he hasn't shared with you... Dev said Jase has demons and doesn't open up to people. Maybe it's not you. Maybe it's just the way he is. If you care about him, don't give up. Fight for him and keep scaling the walls. He'll stop building them up when he feels like he can trust you."

"Trust me?" she cried. "I haven't done anything to make him think he can't."

"Whatever is going on with Jase goes back before you two started seeing each other. You just said you guys were just having fun. Maybe he feels like you don't want to see the deeper side of him. Maybe he needs more of a commitment?"

"I don't know," she slumped down on her elbow. "Something or someone really messed him up in the past. I think the undercover work is just making it worse. He needs to talk to someone and let all of it out."

"Maybe, but I think what he really needs is for someone to fight for him. He needs someone that wants the tomorrows, not just the todays. Show him you're not going anywhere," I smiled as I stood and rounded the bar. I wrapped her in my arms and murmured, "You're good for him Tiff. I've seen the way he looks at you. Don't give up on him."

"Thanks," she sighed as she pulled out of my arms. "I needed that."

"Any time. Now, we need to talk about hiring more people. I can't keep doing this," I groaned as I walked over to the front door and locked it. After flipping the sign to closed, I flicked the lights off, and began heading toward the back.

"Go through those applications this weekend, and let me know if anyone sounds good. I want to start the interview process next week," I called when I reached the back door.

"You got it," she smiled as she followed me out into the parking lot. "Have a nice Thanksgiving," she waved as she jogged over to her car, climbed in, and pulled out of the parking lot.

oooooooooo

When I got home that night, I felt like a Popsicle. It was freezing out, and I'd forgotten my gloves at home. My mom was sound asleep on the couch when I walked in. I gently roused my mother; she'd been so good about helping lately with Mara. With Dev working the night shift, we had texted a few times throughout the night updating each other, and the last one he'd sent said he'd be home around two, he thought.

"She wanted to wait up for you tonight, but I convinced her to get some sleep," my mother smiled as she pointed toward Mara's cracked bedroom door. "She got used to you being here, and she misses you."

I smiled, hugged my mom, and reassured her that I'd spend some extra time with her over the next few days. As I held open the door for her, I reminded her that I'd see her in two days when we celebrated the holidays. She nodded then disappeared down the hall.

I'm not sure how long it took me, minutes maybe, but as soon as I'd locked up I began peeling my smelly bar clothes off and leaving a trail behind me as I made my way to the bedroom. I was exhausted, and all I could think about was taking a quick shower and climbing into bed.

Thoughts of my busy night and the problems Tiff had divulged washed away after I climbed into the shower and stood under the warm spray. My muscles ached from not being used to the work I'd performed all evening. That little bit of time I'd taken off after my accident had totally messed with me. I had to condition myself all over again. I quickly shampooed my hair, scrubbed the bar filth from my body before stepping out, and wrapping myself in a soft plush towel. My eyes were so close to closing on their own that I decided to forgo the PJs, and just climbed into bed. My tired body sank into the soft mattress as I curled around the extra pillow Dev had been sleeping on. The smell of his cologne wafted into my nose causing me to sigh as my eyes fluttered shut and I drifted off into a deep sleep.

I don't know how long I stayed that way, but sometime later, I felt the bed dip. A hard warm body pressed into my back as a muscled arm wrapped around my stomach. I mumbled as my current dream began to fade, and reality sank in. The warm body was real. It wasn't just in my mind.

"Sorry it's so late," he whispered into my ear as his hand ran up my stomach and cupped my breast. "I tried to get out as soon as I could, but the crazies come out during the holidays and the snow makes it worse."

"Mmmm," I moaned as I pressed my hips back into him. I felt him grow against my backside as his fingers began to knead my breast and his trailed light kisses up my neck.

"I thought maybe you were too tired," he murmured as he nipped my ear.

"Mmmm," I slowly shook my head as I turned it in search of his mouth. When I felt our lips connect, I groaned. I'd been waiting for this for over a week, and the fact that I didn't have to stop us was fueling the fire that was building in my belly.

Dev growled as he shifted so his erection slipped right between my thighs. His hips rocked against me as the hand that was cupping my breast began to trail down my stomach. His fingers brushed between my thighs and caused tremors to run through me. The lack of physical intimacy while I'd healed had caused me to become more responsive, and Dev was taking full advantage. "Tell me if I hurt you," he commanded as he grabbed my knee and moved my leg behind him. "I want this to feel good for both of us," his breath tickled my neck as his fingers went back to torturing me.

I nodded as one finger dipped in," Don't stop!" I panted. A second finger joined the assault, and I ground my hips back into him. "So good," I gasped as I reached behind me in search of the steel that was throbbing against my thigh. "I need you so much," I panted as I wrapped my fingers around him. "Please," I begged as I gripped him.

A groaned bubbled up his throat as he removed his fingers and reached for my wrist. After pinning my arms in front of me, he shifted his hips, so he was right at my entrance. "Please!" I begged again. "No more waiting."

Before I could say anything else, he rocked forward, sinking into me. "Fuck," he muttered as he pushed forward a little further. I sighed before grinding my hips back causing him to tense.

"Stop!" he growled as he gripped my hip and held me in place. I grinned in the dark at his lack of ability to hold on before rocking back against his grip. "Sam," he warned as I giggled and shook my hips. "You are fucking asking for it baby."

"Stop holding back and fuck me," I moaned as he slipped even deeper, seating himself all the way to the hilt.

"Shit!" he growled before pulling back slightly and slamming back into me. "You are going be the death of me," he muttered as he rolled us slightly so he could grab the headboard. I grabbed the pillow in front of me to muffle my cries as he pounded into me while muttering things I couldn't understand. His muscles tensed as he worked us so close to the edge and stopped. Every time I was about to fall over the cliff, he would pause, and I would sink back. Finally, after the third time he stopped moving, I took over.

"Fuck, Sam," he growled. "I want this to last."

"We've got five days before I work again. Stop holding back," I reached back and grabbed his hips. His body shook with tension before he started moving again. This time when we got close to the edge, he didn't stop. His hip jacked forward harder and harder until I felt him swell impossibly bigger and explode inside me. Our bodies, slick with sweat, sagged against one another as he held my back to his chest. I sighed contently as he chuckled.

"Feel better," his voice cracked at the end and I could tell, even the dark, he was smirking at me.

"Oh yeah," I giggled as I wiggled my backside against him.

"Sam," he warned as he wrapped his arm around my waist. "I can't recover that quickly."

I giggled as I tried to turn in his arms. He slipped from me as he softened, and when I rolled over, I placed my head on his chest. I could hear his heart thundering where my cheek rested, and the thumping was slowly lulling me to sleep. I yawned as I settled my hand on his stomach and traced the lines of his abs. "Move in with me." It slipped out so quietly that I wasn't sure if he heard it.

"Are you sure?" he mumbled. "You don't have to ask me just because of what we just did."

"No, I want you here. Move in— this weekend. I'll help." I yawned again as my eyes drifted closed.

"I'd love that," he murmured as he craned his neck to press a kiss to the top of my head. I lifted it and smiled. I could barely make out his face in the dark, only the moonlight shone through the single window in my room. "I love you," I whispered as I pressed my mouth to his. "I love you, too," he whispered back as a sigh escaped him. "Get some sleep. We'll talk in the morning."

"It is morning," I giggled as I pointed to the alarm clock that was glowing on the nightstand.

"Go to sleep, Sam," he chuckled as his arm tightened around me.

"So bossy," I murmured as I placed my head back on his chest and let exhaustion take me under.

Chapter 20

When I woke up the next morning, I could sense that I was alone. I reached out and swept my arm across the mattress before opening my eyes. When I didn't feel anything but rumpled sheets, I sighed. This was getting old. Dev never stuck around in bed. After the one morning that Mara caught us, he'd made sure that he was up every day before she was.

I rolled onto my back and blinked at the ceiling a few times before letting my mind wander. Did we really agree to live together last night? Was that real? It sure felt real, but so much of my reality had felt like a dream lately. I was sure I needed to pinch myself so I could wake up.

Things like this never happened for me. I didn't get the guy in the fairy tale.

What were we anyway? We were happy. However, was I just waiting for the inevitable downfall? Dev really hadn't mentioned our relationship status in quite some time. Were we pretending? Was he here out of some sort of obligation to Mara? I didn't think so, but we really hadn't discussed 'us' in a while. The fact that he'd agreed to move in with me should have been a clue as to where things were going, but my muddled brain hadn't processed that yet.

"Mommy?" Mara's voice was timid as she softly knocked on my closed bedroom door. I'd told her that she couldn't just barge in, and she'd been doing really well remembering that lately. Although, Dev was probably out there with her, so I wasn't sure what was going on.

"You can come in," I called as I finished slipping one of Dev shirts on over my head and settled back against the soft pillows.

When the door opened, Mara stood in the doorway grinning, with Dev behind her holding a tray.

"Daddy and I made you breakfast in bed," she giggled as she skipped over to the bed and climbed into is. It was awkward watching her fumble with her cast, but we'd agreed to let her try things on her own, and she was doing surprisingly well.

"You did?" I smiled at her before sending a confused look in Dev's direction. "What's the occasion?"

Mara bounced a few times before settling next to me, "Daddy says today is a special day, and we needed to celebrate." Mara snagged a piece of toast off the tray that Dev had placed in front of me. She nibbled on it before turning toward him, "So what is it?"

"What's what?" I lifted the mug of hot coffee and took a sip.

"I told her we needed to discuss something with her today," he smirked and winked at me.

"I'm confused," I mumbled around the edge of my mug.

Mara giggled as she watched us, and Dev's mouth opened and shut a few time as if he couldn't believe that I didn't know what he was talking about. Finally, he sighed and looked over at our daughter, "Mommy and I talked about something last night, and I wanted to see what you thought."

"What? What? What?" she bounced harder in her excitement.

"How would you feel if Daddy moved in here with you guys?"

I stared, completely taken by the fact that he would even consider asking her. It was so heartfelt and unnecessary. I knew the answer before she even uttered the words.

"Here?" Mara's head tipped to the side.

"Yep," he grinned at her excitement.

"Where would you put your stuff?" she scratched her chin, deep in thought.

"Well," Dev shrugged. "I was planning to put the big stuff in storage and only bring the small things."

"And where would that go?" she scanned the room.

"I could share some of my space with him," I smiled at Mara, "just like I shared space with Andy in Vegas."

Dev tensed beside me at the mention of Andy, but at the moment, I was trying to help my daughter understand what was going on. Thoughts of him being upset were the least of my worries.

"Where would you sleep?" she looked over at the rumpled pillow on my bed.

"Well," he swallowed, and I thought I might have seen him slightly blush.

I couldn't help but laugh at this point. Dev was getting embarrassed by a three year old. Deciding that he'd floundered enough, I jumped in, "He'd stay in here with me."

"Really?" she clapped her hands. "Like a real Mommy and Daddy?"

"What are you talking about, baby?" I watched her excitement waver slightly. "We're still a real Mommy and Daddy even if Daddy doesn't sleep here."

"That's not what Jeremy said," she stuck her lip out. My mother had mentioned this kid at pre-school bothering Mara, but she'd told me she'd taken care of it. Apparently, my daughter needed to hear this from me, too. "Jeremy said that Mommies and Daddies have to sleep in the same bed. He said that's how you get more babies."

"Whoa!" Dev's eyes bugged out as his head jerked up from where it had been staring at his lap.

"Who said anything about more babies?" I questioned as I placed my hand on her shoulder.

"I want a sister," Mara grumbled.

Dev's shoulders shook with laughter as he gave me an amused smile. It was starting to make a little more sense now. She wanted a sibling, that's where this was coming from. "Sweetie," I took a deep breath. "Daddy's gonna move in here and live with us, but Mommy's not ready for another baby yet. We need to get used to just the three of us first. Mommy and Daddy have to talk and decide when babies come. It doesn't just happen."

"But..." she stuck her lip out.

"But we'll let you know when, ok?" Dev watched her, hoping she'd accept the answer he'd given.

"Ok," she shrugged. "I'm going to go watch cartoons," she scrambled down from the bed and took off down the hall.

"Let her know?" I gasped after she ran away.

"Well," he shrugged as he slid closer to me and moved the tray of food to the floor. "I always wanted a large family with lots of kids running around." He placed a kiss on my shoulder, "I missed everything with her. I can't go back, but in the future," he placed his palm on my flat stomach, "I'd like to see you swollen with my child in there."

"Dev," I swallowed before glancing at him. "I'm not ready for another child. yet."

"I know, but it doesn't mean we can't talk about it," he murmured. "I just want you know that if it ever happens, I'll be happy about it. You don't have to worry about that."

I grinned before turning my head in his direction, "You know, just because I'm not ready doesn't mean we can't practice?"

"I like the way you think," he chuckled "but I've got a couple of guys from the station meeting me at my place in an hour, so if you want to help move me in here, we really don't have time right now. Get dressed, and we'll finish this tonight."

"Deal," I giggled.

oooooooooo

After calling my mom and asking her to watch Mara for few hours, we'd made our way up to his loft. He hadn't really lived there over the past month. Most of his everyday things like clothes had been slowly making their way into my place. Things like pictures and small trinkets had to be packed. Dev was busy helping the guys lift things like the couch and kitchen table, and I was boxing the small stuff. He'd already made two trips to his storage locker and was getting ready to make a third when he came over to where I was sitting by the bed.

"We're going to grab some lunch on this next trip, do you want anything, or are you just going to go downstairs to your place?" He squatted down in front of me.

"What are you getting?" I mumbled absentmindedly as I scanned the floor around me.

"Probably just some burgers or something," he shrugged.

"Sure, grab me whatever. I'm just going to finish boxing up all this stuff," I motioned to the bedroom space.

"Ok," he chuckled as he pushed off his knees and shoved himself to a standing position. "I'll be back in a little bit."

"See ya," I called without looking up. I was engrossed in boxing the bedroom items and wasn't really paying attention. I hadn't opened several drawers yet. I felt like I was on a treasure hunt. I'd been in here before, but other than that one time when I first snooped around his place, I really hadn't delved into it. Back then, it was Brian I was trying to figure out. Dev had hidden anything that would lead to his identity. All identification had been locked away in a safe in his closet. Now that I knew who he was, and he wasn't on a job, I could dig until my heart was content.

I didn't really find anything out of the ordinary until I reached the footlocker tucked under his bed. I honestly don't think I would have noticed it if I hadn't been in the process of taking the bed apart. I'd already pulled all the sheets and the comforter off. Now that it was just the frame and mattress, you could clearly see that something was stored underneath.

Curiosity got the better of me, and I tugged on one of the handles until it slid out. It was heavy. The lock popped open with ease, and I grinned as I lifted the lid to see what treasure awaited me. My smile faltered slightly as I peered down inside. The trunk was filled with smaller boxes, all of them labeled with names. I lifted one on the top and read the name Marcus. I opened it and peered inside to find an entire life. A driver's license with Dev's picture and the name Marcus Banks was on top. An employee badge for a business I'd never heard of was lying next to it, then several documents. Dev's messy handwriting was scrolled across several papers. It looked like maybe notes. There were dates and names of places with numbers beside them and at the bottom what looked like surveillance photos. Reality of what I'd found began to creep in as I lifted another box, this one with the name Zach Wright on it.

He had a box like mine, only his was bigger. My past lives fit in a shoe box, just a couple of driver's licenses. I'd been doing this three times longer than he had, and mine fit in one small box. He had at least a dozen lives packed away in here, and the more I read, the more worried I became about the future. Dev had never shared any of this with me, and as I read over the name Brian Sellers, I gasped. With trembling hands, I lifted the box. I held it in my lap and traced the letters with my index finger. Did I want to know what was inside? I did, but I was scared at the same time. This was the one person in this whole box that I knew.

I lifted the lid and peered in. On top was the license that Dev had shown that very first time he came into The Rusty Nail. A credit card was next; I'd seen that, too. The name of the tattoo parlor down the street was scribbled on a scrap of paper, that must have been where he got inked, but what I found tucked near the bottom took my breath away.

Photos… tons of them… all of me. Some were from after we'd met at the bar, those I expected, but there were so many more. Pictures from when I was younger, some not even from Chicago. I gasped when I ran across one that was of my entire family having a picnic in the park. My hand shook as I turned it over to read the writing on the back. There scrolled in handwriting that I didn't recognize were the words "Target and Family".

I turned the photo back over and let my fingers run across the image of my father as he sat on a blanket smiling at me. I could remember the day this was taken; we'd left California that night. The Feds determined that we'd been found once again. George had been relentless, and I was holding the proof. Why did Dev have this and how had he gotten it? More importantly, why he hadn't told me was baffling.

A singled tear slipped down my face as I shuffled through the photos examining each one. I was angry that he had these and hadn't bothered to tell me, but I think I might have been more hurt than anything.

I didn't hear the door open when Dev and the guys came back. I didn't hear anything; I was lost in my memories until he stumbled to a stop in front of me. "Shit!" he hissed when he saw what I was holding.

"Why?" I tipped my chin up so I could look him in the eyes. "Why do you have pictures of my family?"

He glanced over where the two of his buddies were standing and they exchanged silent nods before disappearing outside, then he turned back to me, "It was part of the job."

"You knew they were after me? Why didn't you tell me that you knew who I was when we met?" I sniffed as a feeling of betrayal settled in.

"Sam," he sighed. "I didn't know you were her," he pointed at the picture "not at first, anyway." He shifted and sat down beside me as he reached for the box in my hand, "When I went under with George's group, I knew they were after a family. He gave me those photos. His goons had being doing surveillance on your family for years. He wanted me know who I was after. I kept them in case I ever found that girl, but honestly, I'd forgotten that I had them. When I met you in the bar that night, I didn't know that was you. You looked like her, but I wasn't sure. The more pictures George gave me, the more I put the pieces together."

"When did you know?" I wiped at my eyes and chewed my lip.

"When he gave me this one," Dev dug around in the pile until he found what he was looking for and handed it to me.

When I saw what it was, I gasped, "Oh my god!" There, sitting in my lap, was a photo of Dev and me walking home from school when we were dating in New York. I was Emily then, and he was my boyfriend. "This is you!" I looked up wide-eyed.

"Yes," he nodded.

"No one figured out who you were?" I wrinkled my forehead as I stared at it. We looked so happy and young.

"No," he sighed. "My hair was longer there, and I always kept a slight beard when I was working for George. They handed me that photo the night I left your place right after I found your box of IDs. I knew then that I had to get you out and fast."

I watched him for a minute, not really sure what to do. "Are you mad?" he stared at me. "About all that?" he motioned toward the box.

I looked from the pile of stuff to him only pausing for a second before launching myself into his arms, "Thank you," I cried, as I wrapped my arms around his neck.

"For what?" he mumbled.

"For saving me," I buried my face in his tee shirt clad chest. "I don't think I'd be where I am if you hadn't taken him down."

"It wasn't just me," he chuckled. "We had an entire team."

"I know, but they could have killed you. They showed you photos of yourself, and you held it together. I don't know how to tell you how that makes me feel." I hugged him tighter.

He paused for a minute before pushing against me to break our connection. I loosened my grip as I tipped my chin to stare into his eyes, confusion written all over my face. "Marry me!" he grinned.

"What?" I gasped as I shook my head trying to make sure I heard him right.

"Marry me. We already practically live together. I'm moving in. We have a child together. We love each other. Hell, look at what we've gone through to be together. What are we waiting for?" He lifted me off his lap and held his hand up as he shuffled on his knees over to the chest of drawers against the wall. He pulled open the bottom drawer and dug around for a second before smiling and shuffling back to stop in front of me. He opened his palm to reveal a small velvet box.

"Ohmygod!" It came out in a rush as my hands flew to my mouth.

"I've had this since right after you left the last time," he smirked. "Samantha Elizabeth Connolly, will you marry me?" he lifted the lid on the box to reveal a beautiful sparkling diamond. It looked to be about a three quarter carat square cut with several smaller diamonds nestled around it.

"Dev," the tears that I'd been holding on to were streaming down my face as I darted my eyes between the ring and his face. "I don't know what to say," I murmured.

"Yes would be a good start," he chuckled.

I began to laugh though the tears before I threw myself into his arms once again, "Yes! Yes, I'll marry you!"

He joined in on my laughter as he plucked the ring from its satin confines and slid it on my finger before attacking my mouth in a blistering kiss. We were just about to take things further when a clearing of a throat behind us caused us to jump apart.

"You two can do that later," Jase called as he moved closer, "and congratulations!"

"Thanks," I giggled before turning to face Dev. "We'll pick up where we left off tonight," I whispered as I leaned in next to his ear. "I promise."

He grumbled before standing to follow Jase. I, on the other hand, sat grinning like a fool as I admired my new jewelry. No way did I picture today taking this turn, but I wasn't going to complain. I'd found over the years that the best things were always unplanned.

Chapter 21

Thanksgiving morning was anything but normal. The turkey I'd been defrosting in the fridge for the last two days was still frozen, Dev had been called into work the night before, had yet to get back home, and Mara had been whining about playing in the snow since the minute she got up. I'd called my mother in a panic begging for help, and thankfully, she rushed over.

"Thank god!" I threw open the door anxiously, the minute my mother knocked on it.

"Calm down!" she laughed as she shook her head at me. "Everyone has at least one year like this in their life. It'll be ok."

"No it won't," I whined. "I wanted this year to be perfect. I closed the bar so I could concentrate on this and looked what happened."

"Sam," she laughed again as she maneuvered her way into the condo. She was carrying a large container in her hands, and she struggled as she moved to place it in my kitchen.

"What's that?" I pointed as I closed the door behind her.

"A turkey," my mother sighed before turning to face me, "and before you say anything, no, I did not plan for you to fail."

"How did you happen to have one then?" I crossed my arms over my chest and scowled.

"It's not cooked," she pushed a few buttons on my stove. "I was planning to have some friends over tomorrow and this was for that. I'll switch with you, and we can eat this one today," she moved around my kitchen with ease as she began searching the cabinets. She turned and smiled at me, "Are you going to help, or stand there?"

I blew out a breath before throwing my head back in laughter, "Let's do this."

Mom and I spent the next several hours mixing, chopping, sautéing, boiling, and baking all of the dishes I'd so carefully planned. When we finished and stepped back to admire our work I was pleasantly surprised.

"That turned out better than I thought," I grinned at her.

"Better go get cleaned up before your man gets home," my mom smiled at me as she lifted a piece of flour-covered hair from my eyes. I laughed as I glanced down at myself and noticed it was practically covering my clothes.

"Good idea," I untied the apron from my waist and tossed it on the counter. "Keep an eye on her?" I motioned to where Mara was watching a parade on TV. My mother smiled and nodded as I turned and headed for the bathroom.

After cleaning up, dressing, and drying my hair, I made my way back toward the living room. I could hear laughter coming down the hall, and my heart soared. Dev was home. I was surprised that he hadn't come looking for me.

"Happy Thanksgiving," he grinned when I stepped around the corner.

"You, too," I chirped as I twisted my hands in front of me. We hadn't told my mom about our engagement yet, and I had removed my ring before I started cooking. With all the chaos this morning, I'd completely forgotten about telling her. We hadn't told Mara yet either because we wanted to wait and tell her together. With Dev at work last night, we hadn't gotten a chance yet. I knew they'd both be happy, but my nerves were getting the best of me.

"So?" he tilted his head to the side as he stood and rounded the corner. I watched him amble closer and took in his appearance. He looked utterly exhausted. His eyes had dark circles under them, and he was still dressed in his clothes from yesterday. The twinkle that was normally in his eyes was dimmer than usual, and he seemed to have the weight of the world on his shoulders.

"You ok?" I murmured when he was close enough to hear me. He nodded, but it didn't seem very convincing. "You sure about that?"

"It was long night," he mumbled. "We've got a big case that I thought we were close to closing, but apparently I was wrong."

"Mmm, are you going to have to go back tonight?" I reached up to cup his jaw not even thinking about my ring.

He leaned in to me and closed his eyes, "I can't talk about work with you, baby. You know this."

"Sam?" my mother's voice broke me out of my thoughts of Dev. She stood slowly from where she was perched on the couch, and her hand lifted to her mouth as her eyes widened. "Are you? Does this mean?" her words were caught in her throat as she pointed to the two of us and moved closer.

I looked from Dev to her before I figured out what she was talking about. Once I made the connection, I yanked my hand away as I sunk my teeth into my lip. Dev turned, so he was beside me instead of in front me. He wrapped his arm around my waist and tugged me flush to his side.

"Are you two?" My mother had finally reached us, and she grabbed at my hand to stare at the sparkling diamond that sat on my third finger.

"Getting married?" Dev finished for her. She nodded her head vigorously before quickly glancing behind her to see if the smallest ears in the room had heard her. "Yes," Dev smiled as he turned his face and pressed his lips to the top of my head.

"When did this happen?" My mom smiled at the two us.

"Yesterday," I grinned now, happy that she was happy for us.

"And you kept it a secret for that long?" she smirked.

"She's good at keeping secrets," Dev nudged me. I couldn't tell if that statement upset him or not. He was so tired and worn down that I wasn't sure what he was feeling.

"Why don't we eat while it's still hot," I tilted my head toward the table. "I'm sure a certain someone wants some turkey." As soon as the words fell from my lips, Mara bounced up off the couch, "Can we eat now? I'm hungry."

I laughed as I nodded at her and watched her rush to the table. We spent the next few hours talking and laughing as we devoured all the delicious food Mom and I had prepared. Plans to tell Mara about our big news fell to the wayside, as talks of building a snowman were her top priority.

"Can we?" she bounced on the balls of her feet and tugged at Dev's wrist. "Please, Daddy!"

I watched the struggle on his face. He wanted to go with her; I knew he did. The way she had settled into calling him Daddy and asking him for things had come so natural. He was exhausted though. I was honestly surprised that Dev was still awake. I knew with his job that this was nothing new. I'm sure over his career, he'd spent many nights awake and many shifts with no sleep, but I he'd never had a three year old wanting to push his energy to the limits when he did make it home.

"Sweetie," I reached for Mara. "Daddy's really tired. Maybe we can do something in here tonight and build a snowman tomorrow?" I tried to capture her attention, but she wasn't having it.

"It's no fair!" she stomped her little foot and awkwardly crossed her arms. "You're never here!"

"Mara!" I scolded. I hadn't seen her act like this in a while, but it wasn't unheard of. Her world had been flipped on its side over the last few months, and she'd been rolling with the punches pretty well. I knew that it wouldn't last forever, and I'd been silently wondering when the typical three-year-old behavior that I had known back in Vegas would make an appearance.

"It's ok," Dev sighed as a yawn escaped him.

"No, it's not," I shook my head. "She knows better."

"Sam," he reached across the table and placed his hand over mine. "Really, it's ok." I watched him slowly drag himself to an upright position and shuffle over to the door. He lifted the coat that he'd tossed on the back of a chair and began tugging it on.

"What are you doing?" I gasped.

"Building a snowman with my daughter," he offered a weak, tired smile.

"Dev, no. She needs to learn that she can't always get what she wants," I shook my head as I watched him tie his boots.

"Not today she doesn't," he slipped his gloves on and then reached for Mara's hand. She'd been pouting while she was half-dressed. All that had remained left to do was slip on her boots. "We'll be back shortly," he called as he opened the door and slipped into the hallway.

"You've got a good man there," my mother smiled at me as she stood and began taking dirty dishes into the kitchen.

"Yeah," I agreed as I blew out a breath. "He's gonna spoil her though."

"He's missed a lot," my mom called as she disappeared into the kitchen. "Don't be too hard on him."

When Dev and Mara finally came back inside, my mother said her goodbyes and headed home with the turkey that I hadn't cooked. I thanked her for all her help and promised to update her as soon as we had set a date for the wedding. I knew we didn't want to wait, but we hadn't really thought much further than that.

After Mara stripped out of her snowy clothes, I gave her a bath and tucked her in. I had left Dev on the couch watching football and had little hope that he'd be awake when I returned. Sure enough, when I rounded the corner he was stretched out on the couch. Half his body was hanging off like he'd literally just flopped down. His shoes and coat were all he'd managed to get off. His face looked so peaceful as he lay there snoring softly. His hair was in disarray from the snow hat he'd been wearing most of the day. His cheeks were red from the winter wind, and his lips were pursed as if he was deep in thought.

"Hey," I nudged him slightly. I didn't want to wake him, but I knew that he'd be more comfortable in bed. "Hey," I tried again, and this time his eyes blinked rapidly like he was trying to clear the sleep from them. "Let's go to bed," I swung my head toward the bedroom door.

Without speaking, he nodded, yawned, and pushed himself up. I watched as he brushed his teeth before stripping down to his boxers and climbing into bed. Something was off today. It was like he had been putting on a show while my mother was here, and now the burden of whatever happened at work was finally catching up and taking its toll.

"Are you ok?" I whispered as I clicked off the light and snuggled under the covers next to him.

"I'm fine," he mumbled.

"You don't seem fine," I reached up and laid my palm on his bare shoulder.

"I've got a lot going on," he sighed.

"Wanna talk about it?" I pushed.

"I can't," anger seeped into his voice as he rolled to his side. "Please stop asking me to."

"I'm sorry," I murmured. "I just… never mind," I grumbled as I laid there staring at the ceiling in the dark.

"Don't do this," he huffed. "Don't get mad at me because I can't tell you something. I'm trying here, Sam. I'm being as honest as I can about myself."

"I know," I mumbled. "It doesn't mean I have to like it."

He took a deep breath and paused before shifting to face me, "I love you. I'll talk to you in the morning. I think we both need some sleep right now."

"I love you, too. Good night," I whispered as I turned away from him. I didn't want him to see the tears that were silently slipping from my eyes as I questioned whether this was going to work. I didn't want him to know that the things I worried about seemed to be real now that he was back at work. I hoped more than anything that the anxiety that I felt was unfounded and he really wasn't hiding anything big from me, but later that night when his phone rang, and he slipped from our bed, I knew my fears were real. I knew the minute I heard the door click shut, when he slipped out into the night, that the worries I been imagining were nothing compared to what was coming my way in the future.

Chapter 22

Over the next three days, my mood didn't improve. Dev had been practically nonexistent in our lives. He came home to sleep, but other than that, you'd never know he'd moved in. Mara hadn't really seemed to notice, or if she had, she didn't say anything. My mother had kept quiet the last few times we'd talked as I ranted about how unfair it all was.

Tonight was the first night that the bar was reopening after the holiday break, and I was trying with everything in me to be normal. Tiff had called me in a panic this morning about the liquor order. It seems that they messed up the delivery date, and she wasn't sure we'd have enough this week. The holidays seemed to bring out the drinkers, and with the local colleges going on winter break, we were going to be swamped.

"What are we going to do?" she rushed over as I stepped through the back door and shook the snow off my coat.

"We'll be fine," I began unwrapping myself from all the layers. "I've got a reserve in the basement we can pull from."

"What?" Tiff's eyes flashed. "What reserve?"

I laughed as I began turning on lights and unlocking the door to my secret hideaway, "I put some away when we first opened for occasions just like this. Shit happens," I shrugged. "I wanted to be prepared."

"This is the first time I've ever been happy about you being paranoid," she giggled as she followed me.

"See, I knew you loved me," I teased as I turned on the light at the bottom of the steps. "Voilà," I waved my arms toward the stack of boxes to our right. "Take whatever we need. I'll fill this back up next week when the truck comes."

"This is where I'm going to start taking my breaks," Tiff murmured as she lifted two bottles into her arms.

"I might move in here," I responded sarcastically. "Wanna be my roommate?"

"I don't think Dev would like that," she giggled.

"I don't really care," I snapped back.

Tiff spun and placed the bottles on the ground beside her. She crossed her arms and began tapping her foot. "Spill!" she cocked her head to the side.

"I'm not doing this now," I turned and began stomping up the stairs. When I rounded the corner, I noticed Mason and Chris were setting up for the night and Courtney was tying her apron around her waist. "Are we ready?" I glanced at the three of them.

"You've got a line at the door," Mason chuckled as he nodded to the small crowd had gathered.

"Guess they missed us," I laughed. I was glad that all of my regular staff was able to work tonight. I was tired of having to fill in for people, and I actually wanted to play the part of the owner. "Unlock the doors and let them in," I pointed to Mason. "Showtime!" I clapped as I turned just in time to see Tiff. She was glaring at me, probably over the way I'd left things between us, but I really didn't want to talk about it. I'd been mad for days now. I needed to get it out in my own way. Dev was working, and the more I denied it the better I felt about it. I knew things weren't good. I knew that whatever case he was on was doing this, I just couldn't think about it right now. Deep down, I was afraid, but I'd never admit it. What if he left? What if this case took him away? How would I deal with it?

"You ok?" Mason stared at me as he moved to unlock the door.

"I'm fine. Let's do this," I waved my hand in the air as I flicked on the jukebox.

As the night wore on, the hours ticked by quicker than I could have predicted. We ended up having plenty of liquor and Tiff hadn't mentioned Dev again. We'd had a packed house, and several customers had been asking Chris when his band was going play again. I knew having live music was going to be a success, but I couldn't have predicted how successful. I'd told him that if he could find me a bartender as good as he was, he could play any night he wanted. He seemed to take the challenge and promised me a new hire by the end of the week. I had my doubts, but we would see.

"Hey," Tiff nudged me as she wiped at the bar. "Are we going to talk about this now?"

I knew what she meant, and quite frankly, I was surprised that she was pushing the issue, but she was my friend and she knew something was bothering me.

"I know you're probably going to get mad at me, but you were there for me last week and I just want you to know that I'm here for you," she looked at me and I could see the understanding in her eyes.

"I'm just mad," I grumbled.

"Why?" she reached out and touched my shoulder causing me to tense.

"It's stupid, and that just makes me madder," I growled.

"Talk to me," she begged. "I know that's not your thing, but you'll feel better if you do."

"I'm mad at Dev, and I'm mad at myself for being mad at Dev," I took a deep breath and then moved around the bar and found a place to sit. This conversation was going to take a while, and my feet were killing me after the night we'd had.

"Ok," she murmured as she followed me. "Why?"

"He's been distant lately. Never home, and when he is, I can tell he's really not there. His body is, but his head is somewhere else. I can see it in his eyes. He helps with Mara, and does what he can when he's there, but that isn't much. Yesterday, I wouldn't have even known he'd come home if the pillow on his side of the bed hadn't been dented. He comes in after I'm asleep and leaves before I wake. He's on the phone all the time. He thinks I don't know because he's all secretive and quiet, but I feel the bed dip and hear the whispered conversations," I placed my elbows on the table in front of me and let my head drop into my hands. Tiff just nodded silently as she watched me fall apart. "Say something," I muttered.

"Have you talked to him about this?" her voice was quiet, almost timid, like she knew it was a sore subject.

"I tried the first day it happened. He left in the middle of the night right before Thanksgiving. I knew about that one. Then on Thanksgiving Day, he did it again. We'd just gotten into bed. I tried to talk to him and he got mad," I made air quotes, "he said he couldn't talk about work." Tiff nodded some more.

"I'm afraid, Tiff. I'm afraid he's going to be called away again, and he's not going to tell me. I'm afraid he's just not going to come home one night. I'm so angry right now. I'm angry that this happening. I'm angry that it bothers me. I'm really angry that my daughter, his daughter, loves him so much and he might leave us. How am I going to explain that to her? This is what I was afraid of when I let him back in," I was yelling now and had balled my hands into fists that I was slamming down on the table in front of me.

"I'll talk to Jase," she sighed. "Maybe he can tell me something."

"I thought the two of you had stopped hanging out," I looked up at her and wiped at my eyes. Angry tears had been slowly trickling out of the corners for the last ten minutes.

"We aren't really anything at the moment. We had what I thought was going to be a good thing, but he shut me out emotionally," she shrugged and gave a sad smile. "We still talk though. Whatever demons he's facing, he doesn't want me to be a part of it," she pushed back her chair. "They're partners, though. If Dev's hiding something, then Jase will know."

"How do you know he'll tell you?" I offered a watery smile.

"I have my ways," a small smile slipped into place.

"Tiff," I warned.

"What?" she shrugged. "I said he shut down emotionally, not physically."

"What aren't you telling me," I wrinkled my forehead as I watched her slowly make her way over behind the bar. She lifted a bottle of amber liquid and poured two shots. She carefully carried them back to where we were sitting and gently pushed one toward me. "We still hang out and have fun, it's just not what I really had in mind when I started hanging around him," she shrugged and then tossed her head back as she swallowed the liquid. Her eyes pinched shut as she shivered before slamming the shot glass back down. "Your turn," she narrowed her eyes on me.

"I don't think drinking with you is a good idea. It always ends in me feeling like crap the next day," I sighed as I eyed the glass.

"Oh, stop," she groaned. "Mara's with your mom and there are like three other people here who can drive you home."

"What the hell?" I muttered as I lifted the glass to my lips and downed the liquid. It burned like fire and I coughed and sputtered as it made its way into my belly. "What was that?"

"Something new," she grinned before walking back to the bar to grab the bottle. "Want some more," she laughed when she came back.

"What is it?" I reached for the bottle but she yanked it out of my reach before I could get it. "Give me the damn bottle."

"No!" she laughed as she filled the shot glasses once again. "Drink!" she commanded as she downed hers.

The night wore on like this until we were completely shit-faced. I don't know how many shots I took, but the more I poured down my throat, the better I seemed to feel. "Whaaa is thissss stuuffff?" I slurred as I reached for the bottle. Tiff was now drunk enough that her reflexes weren't what they were when we started so I was able to grab the bottle from her. I squinted my eyes as I studied the label trying to read it. What did it say? Fire? Fire what? I turned the bottle in my hands and sniffed it as if that would give me the answer when it was roughly yanked from my grip. "What the hell?" I screeched as my head tipped up to see who'd taken it from me. There, towering over me, was the source of my anger.

"What the fuck are you doing?" Dev growled as he crossed his arms over his chest. His worn jeans looked delicious on him, as did the leather jacket he was wearing. I hadn't seen him dress like this since I'd known him as Brian.

"Whatever the fuck I want!" I attempted to stand, and I wobbled slightly.

"Dude, calm down," another voice sounded from behind me. When I spun around, almost falling back into my seat, I noticed that at some point, Jase had joined this party.

"We're closed," I giggled as I tried to get the bottle back from Dev.

"Yeah, if your buddy Mason hadn't called me, you'd be sleeping here tonight," Dev rolled his eyes. He shifted his stance, and I licked my lips as I watched the muscles in his thighs flex.

"What do you care," I fired back. "You haven't been around enough to notice." Shit! Did I say that out loud? My head was so fuzzy with what was real and what wasn't, that my mouth was having a hard time keeping up and staying closed.

Just then, Tiff's laugh rang out beside me. I turned to see Jase standing behind her whispering something in her ear. Her face lit up and nodded vigorously as she attempted to stand.

"Dude, you got this?" Jase looked from me to Dev before wrapping his arm around Tiff's waist.

"Yeah," Dev nodded. "I'm good."

"Wait," I gasped. "You're just going to go off with him? After everything you told me?"

Tiff's face reddened and Jase's bore a confused scowl. "I'm fine," she hissed as she snaked one arm around his middle and let it trail down the front of pants.

"Damn, woman," Jase gulped. "Let's go before you molest me right here."

"Bye," Tiff giggled as they turned and walked away.

I huffed before looking back at Dev. His eyes were dark with fury as he watched me. I could feel the anger radiating off him. He stalked closer until his chest was pressed against mine, "You wanna tell me what the hell is going on? Why are you suddenly drinking and avoiding me?"

"I can't do this now," I muttered as I refused to make eye contact.

"Why? I thought we were past the secrets. I thought you wanted to move forward with me. Hell, you're wearing my ring," he grabbed my hand and rubbed his thumb across the diamond.

"Secrets?" I lifted my arms and shoved at his chest. "Me? Me keeping secrets?" I screeched as I pushed with all my might. I was pissed, and he'd just woken up the bitch that I'd been drowning in alcohol. "Where the hell do you get off accusing me of keeping secrets? I've been nothing but honest with you since we re-started whatever this is," I waved my hands in the air manically. "I've told you everything. Laid my heart out, and you've been slowly slipping away over the last week."

"What are you talking about?" he roared.

"I hear you when you leave," his posture stiffened as he watched me. "You think I don't know, but I do," I jammed my finger into his chest. "The phone calls, the leaving in the middle of the night. It's like it used to be. Are you leaving? Is that what this is? Are you getting ready to leave us?" I was crying and yelling now, and the alcohol was only fueling my anger. "Just tell me!" I begged as I watched his eyes dart from my eyes, to my lips, to a space above my head.

He stood there without saying a word and his face told me the answer I was looking for. "Whatever you're working on at work," I nodded "it's bad, isn't it?" He sighed and squeezed his eyes shut. "I've seen the other phone. They want you back, don't they?" He looked away, and when his eyes opened, they were filled with anguish. "Oh god," I gasped as I stepped back. "Oh god, oh god, oh god," I muttered as I stumbled toward the bar. "No, no. no. This can't be happening. Not now."

"Baby?" his voice was quiet and unsure, almost as if he was begging me to say it was ok, ok to leave again.

"Tell me I'm wrong," I begged.

"I've been trying to find a way to not have to do this. I don't want to do this, you hear me?" he cupped my jaw as he bent his knees so we were eye level. "I don't want to do this," he stated again as he watched me. "This case... I was on this case before you came back here. I have to finish it."

"When?" I sobbed as I turned away from him.

I knew he knew what I was asking. He sighed before giving a resigned, "Next week."

"Huh?" my head snapped up.

"I leave Monday. I was going to talk to you about it tonight. I knew Mara wasn't going to be home, so I thought we could talk and figure out what we're going to do," he shrugged.

"How long?" I sobbed again.

"Sam," he mumbled.

"How long?" I insisted.

"I don't know," he murmured "A month, maybe six, it depends on how long it takes to close this."

"What about us?" I wiped at my eyes. "What are we supposed to do while you're gone?"

"I'm coming back. I promise. I'm coming back and getting out of the UC unit. This is just a little delay, not a rewrite of the future. I promise… nothing's going to keep me from being with you."

"Promise?" I stood and wrapped my arms around his neck. He sagged in relief against me, "Promise."

Chapter 23

When I slowly began to wake the next morning, my head was throbbing. I cursed myself for drinking so much the night before and vowed never to let it happen again. I was sure that it would, but at the moment, I didn't care if I ever tasted the rancid stuff again. I rolled on to my back and reached out across the bed. I sighed when my arm didn't make contact with anything other than cold sheets. He was gone... again. Tears formed in my eyes as I began to recall the conversation that we'd had the night before. My chest ached, and I couldn't tell if the pounding in my head was coming from the alcohol or all the crying I had done the night before. I vaguely remember Dev holding me and attempting to comfort me as I babbled on about how I was going to go back to doing this alone. He'd assured that nothing was going to keep him away again and it wouldn't be forever.

"Morning," his voice was quiet, and I jumped slightly when I heard him. My eyes blinked a few times as I watched him stand there in the bedroom doorway. He was leaning against the jamb in only a pair of navy police issued sweats holding a mug of coffee.

"So last night— it really happened, didn't it?" I murmured as I turned away from him.

"Yeah," he sighed before shoving off the doorway and shuffling over to sink down on the bed beside me. "Sam," he lowered the mug to the nightstand and shifted to face me. "I love you, you know that. I don't like not being able to tell you stuff, but it's part of this job. I tell you as much as I can. It's tearing me apart to have to keep things from you, but that's just the way it is."

I nodded and pushed myself up so I was sitting in front of him, "I know; I'm just scared."

"I know you are, and I promise that it's not going to be this way forever. This is my last job… I promise. When this is done, I'm going to change units. I'll work locally. I'll be home every night. Well, I'll try to be home every night," he smirked. When I tried to look away, he reached out and grabbed my chin. "Marry me," he leaned in closer so our foreheads were touching.

"I already said yes," I whispered.

"Today," he murmured before pulling back slightly. His eyes moved quickly over my face watching for my reaction. I'd gotten used to his assessments over the last few months. Dev was perceptive. He always knew exactly what I was feeling.

"Today?" I gulped. "But..."

"But nothing. I love you, and I want to marry you. We can go to the courthouse. We'll call your mom, and she can meet us there with Mara. I'll do whatever you want, but why do we need to wait?"

"Dev," I gasped. "I don't have a dress. None of our friends will know about this. You're leaving in three days. This is crazy," I glanced around the room frantically. Was I really considering this?

"I love you," he cupped my face in his hands. "Say yes. Say you'll be my wife... today."

I sat completely still for a few moments as I let the idea tumble around in my head. He was right, what were we waiting for? "Yes," I grinned as the tears fell. "I'll marry you today." I sprung forward causing Dev to lose his balance and fall back against the mattress.

"Ok," he jumped up. "Get dressed. It's going to be a busy day." He reached for his phone and began dialing as he paced around our room. "Yeah, hey man," he nodded. "I'm not coming in tonight. You're gonna have tell the captain. She said yes," he grinned before turning his back to me. "Remember what I asked you last night? Yeah... can you do that for me? Thanks. I owe ya," he clicked the phone off and turned to face me. "Call your mom. Tell her three o'clock," he tossed the phone at me. "Then get yourself ready. Wear that pretty lace dress you've got."

"That's a spring dress. It's snowing outside," I giggled at his excitement.

"I don't care," he shrugged. "You look beautiful in that. Now hurry up. I want to get to the honeymoon part."

"What honeymoon part," I called out confused.

"I booked us something special for tonight. Jase is helping me," he leaned back in the doorway and winked. "Now get your ass in the shower."

"Yes sir," I saluted before scrambling out of the bed. I pushed the fear that had been sitting right below the surface to the back of my mind as I rushed into the bathroom. I knew my time with him was limited, and I wanted to enjoy this. I'd have time to think later after he left. I wasn't sure how much time that would be, but based on last night, I might have six months of it.

ooooooooo

When I look back on this day, I'm not going to remember how rushed I felt, or the fact that it was colder than Antarctica outside. I won't remember that Mara whined about spending the night at Grandma's again, or that I didn't get the reception with all the dancing and partying that I had once pictured. The fact that I didn't have flowers or a long white dress won't matter, either. What will be important is that I'd finally found The One. The one person that loved me, for me. Sam.

The justice of the peace stood before the four of us and recited the typical wedding vows. Did Dev take me and did I take him. My mother and Jase had been our witnesses, and Mara had stood by grinning not really understanding exactly what was going on. We'd told her that we had always been a family, but now we were making it official. Dev had explained as best he could that he was going to be away on business, and he wasn't sure when he'd be back but that he loved us. I know Mara didn't really understand what it all meant, but I could tell by the look on my mother's face that she was worried about me. I would be fine; I knew that. I would carry on like I always had as the strong, confident, woman that I was. Nothing was going to shake that feeling of happiness that had surrounded me when the JOP exclaimed that we were husband and wife.

"Are you sure you don't mind?" I smiled at my mother as she held tight to Mara's gloved hand.

"It's your wedding night. You don't need a three year old tagging along," she chided me as she winked at Dev. "I think your husband might like a little alone time, too."

My husband, that still sounded odd to me and I couldn't help but giggle when Dev agreed. He chuckled before reaching into his pocket and pulling out a small piece of paper. He handed it to my mother and let her know that if she needed us for anything she could call the number that was written on it.

"We'll be back on Monday," I smiled as Dev began dragging me toward his car. We'd parked around the corner, and as we went one way, my mother and Mara went the other.

"Someone seems to be in a hurry," I laughed as he stalked even faster toward the car.

"Someone is ready to consummate this marriage," he growled as he spun me and shoved me back against the side of the car. "I've been waiting since I was seventeen to make you Mrs. Ford," he leaned in so his mouth was almost touching mine before he whispered against my lips, "I'm tired of waiting." I sighed as his mouth came down on mine and I felt every muscled inch press against me. One hand cupped my head while the other gripped my hip firmly. When he broke the kiss, he rested his forehead on mine, "We need to get out here before I take you right up against this car."

"Well, let's go then," I grinned as I moved my head back so I could look directly in his eyes.

Dev growled as he pushed back and opened my door. After climbing in, he jogged around to the driver's side, hopped in, and took off down the street. He drove us right into the center of downtown before turning into The Trump International Hotel. "What are we doing?" I gasped as he turned to grin at me.

"Checking in," he shrugged as he pulled up to the valet.

"We can't afford this," I hissed as I glanced around frantically.

"Yes we can. It was a gift," he pushed open his door and climbed out. I sat there for a minute letting it all sink in on where we were exactly. This place was above his pay grade so how the hell could he afford it? "You coming, or are you going to sleep in the car?" he smirked at me as he leaned back in after handing his keys to the attendant.

I swallowed, "I'm coming. I'm afraid to ask where the money for this came from," I muttered as I climbed out and yanked my small overnight bag out behind me.

Dev sighed, "I work with a guy whose parents are well off. He asked them for a favor."

"Why does someone who comes from that kind of money work as a cop?" I narrowed my eyes on him.

"Sam," he reached for me, and tugged me after him as he headed into the lobby. "Did you ever think that not everyone wants to do what their parents want them to? Jeff didn't want to go into the family business," he shrugged. "Enjoy this, and stop worrying. We've got three days to do nothing but relax and enjoy one another."

"Fine," I leaned into his side and nuzzled his neck. "Let's get our room key, and place the Do Not Disturb sign on the door."

"Deal," he winked. "I've been dying to get you naked anyway."

It didn't take us long to get up to our room. Dev had rushed me along as soon as he had the key card. I think if we'd been alone in the elevator, he would have stripped me right there.

"You know we're not leaving this room all weekend, right?" he pushed the door open and ushered me in. "No phones, no work, no visitors, nothing but you and me." He let the door close behind him and yanked at his tie. "I hate these things," he tossed it to the side as he started fighting with his suit jacket.

"I think you look sexy." I sauntered over to stand in front of him and placed my hands flat on his chest. "Come to think of it, I've never seen you look sexier. I like this look," I reached up and began unbuttoning his shirt.

"Really?" he smirked. "You like this better than what's underneath?"

"Well," I shrugged. "Nothing can beat what's underneath." When I got to the last button, I gently tugged the shirt free from his pants and pushed it off his shoulders. It fluttered to the ground, and as I stood there watching his chest rise and fall with ragged breaths, I could feel my own insides tightening. I swallowed before skimming my knuckles down his chest and abs and stopping at his belt. "This needs to go, too," I murmured as I slowly began working the clasp free.

"Seems like it's a little unfair here," he mused. "Here I am, almost naked, and you're still dressed. I might have to arrest you for accosting me."

"Huh?" I slid the belt from his pants and dropped it to the floor. When I went for the clasp of his slacks, I heard what sounded like metal jingling. I scrunched my nose up as I patted against his pocket. Maybe the apartment keys were in there. I sucked in a breath when I reached in and felt the cool metal of his cuffs.

"Thought we could have a little fun," he grinned as he wrapped his fingers around my wrist and pulled it from his pocket. My eyes darted up to meet his, and the love there had turned to a deep hunger.

"Fun," I slanted my head to the side. Two could play this game. I leaned up on tiptoes and pressed my lips to his in a searing kiss. When my tongue swept into his mouth, my hand dipped back into his pocket. I quickly grabbed the cuffs and stepped back away from him causing him to lose his balance momentarily.

"Samantha," he warned as his eyes bored into mine and darkened even more.

"Devlin," I grinned as I nibbled on my lip and twirled the cuffs around my index finger.

"I'll let you have your fun," he stepped closer, "but I get to have mine when you're finished." He sat down on the end of the bed and lifted his arms in front of himself to show his compliance.

I nodded as I moved closer and stood in front of him. After instructing him to slide up the bed, I linked the cuffs through the headboard before cuffing his wrists around it. He tugged a few times as if he actually thought he could get free before giving a resigned sigh. "They're police issue," I giggled. "Do you really think you can get out of them?"

He smirked, but kept his mouth closed and just watched me. I moved over to where the window was and glanced out at the night sky. It really was pretty, and the snow that had been falling earlier in the day had created a white blanket over everything. All the signs of a long winter were written over every surface.

"Samantha," Dev grumbled. "You've got me all tied up. What are you going do now?"

"Didn't anyone ever teach you patience, Mr. Ford?" I turned and reached behind my back to pull the zipper of my dress down. I let it pool around my ankles as Dev released a hiss. "Good things come to those who wait," I pouted as I climbed up on the bed and straddled his knees. With both hands, I grabbed the waistband of his boxers and began tugging them down, releasing his cock from its confines. I couldn't help but lick my lips when it stood there hard and proud ready for me.

"You're killing me woman," he groaned as I leaned down and let my breath blow across the tip. "Fuuuccckk!" he hissed as his hips rocked up off the bed. I giggled as I leaned closer and wrapped one hand around the base.

"Is this what you want?" I taunted as leaned impossibly closer and ran my tongue up the underside.

"Shit yeah!" he gasped. "Feels... so... good," he panted as I moved my other hand from the bed to place it on his thigh. His muscles were so tense that I thought he was literally going to break. Before any more words slipped from his lips, I sank down on him, taking him as far as I could into my mouth. He was warm and velvety and had that purely Dev smell. His hips rocked up again as if he was trying to climb further into me. "Sam," he panted, "Fuck I want to touch you," he pulled at his bound wrists and caused the bed to shake. "Let me loose," he begged.

"Un un," I muttered as I swallowed and caused him to hiss again. I could feel him losing control as I let him slip from my mouth creating a popping noise. I began climbing up his body placing kisses all along his stomach, chest, and neck before reaching his mouth.

"You should be a fucking interrogator," he muttered and then groaned when I sat and slid my center over him, sinking down, and taking him in in one movement. "Fuck, you're gonna pay for not letting me touch you," he growled but I silenced him as I leaned over and connected our lips in another frantic kiss. I rocked against him and used my hands for leverage against his chest as I bounced faster and harder. "Oh god I'm gonna come," I tossed my head back as a jolt surged through my body. It felt as if lightening had struck me causing every muscle to twist and tighten. Dev followed soon after with a few shouts and gasps as his hips surged up off the bed before he collapsed against the pillows.

"I love you so much," I panted as I tried to catch my breath. I was still lying on top of Dev, and his chest vibrated with laughter. "What?" I lifted my head to look into his eyes. I couldn't understand what could possibly be so funny.

"Could you grab the key out of my pants pocket?" he tugged his hands causing the bed to shake again.

I smiled at him, "I kinda like having you tied up." I slid off him and stood there beside the bed just taking in the scene. We were a sweaty mess, and Dev had several marks on his arms and chest from me. "Crap," I rubbed lightly at a bite mark. "Did I hurt you?"

"Are you really asking me that?" he snickered.

"I don't know what came over me," I muttered as I reached for his discarded pants and searched for the key. When I found it, I carefully unlocked the cuffs, and set them on the night table before turning back to face Dev. He had his arms crossed behind his head and a proud smile on his lips. "What?" I laughed and furrowed my brow.

"I didn't know my wife could be so controlling in the bedroom," he shrugged before he sprung up catching me off guard. He wrapped his arms around me and turned quickly so that I was on my back. "I like it," he snickered before he leaned down and covered my body with his. "And now I want to touch it," his hand blindly searched around until he made contact with what he was looking for causing my eyelids to flutter closed.

"Touch away," I mumbled as I let him have his way with me. I would never tire of this. Dev knew exactly what to do to bring me to the point of insanity. He knew when to boss me around, and when to let me take control. He knew me better than anyone.

We spent the next three days pleasing each other in every way we knew how. We'd made love on every surface in our room multiple times, and when the time came to head back to reality, we both were having a hard time accepting it.

"How will I know you're ok?" I whispered as we stood in the doorway of my apartment, which was now our apartment. Dev had his 'go bag' slung over his shoulder.

"You know I can't call you," his voice was quiet. "But if you need anything at all, or anything happens, call this number," he placed a card in my hand with a handwritten phone number on it. "That's Eric's direct number. Calling him is the best way to reach me on this assignment. He's my handler, and can get a message to me if it's an emergency." I nodded numbly as I fingered the card. This feeling was all too familiar as we stood there. "I know this sucks, but it won't be for long and I promise that this is it. When I get back, I'm getting out. You, me, and Mara... we're going to be a family. I promise," he leaned down and pressed his lips to mine. I closed my eyes and wrapped my arms around his neck squeezing him tight. I could feel tears trickling down his cheeks, which only caused mine to fall harder.

"I love you," I cried as I squeezed tighter. "Please be careful, and come back to us as soon as you can."

"I will," he whispered as he pressed a kiss to my jaw. "I love you, too." He pushed back and nodded one last time before turning on his heel and heading for the elevator.

I held the sob in as long as I could, but when my daughter came up behind me and wrapped her arms around my legs, I couldn't take it anymore. I sank down and wrapped my arms around her.

"It's ok, Mommy," Mara soothed. "Daddy's coming back real soon. He told me so, and then we're going to all be together."

"That's right, baby," I wiped at my eyes. "Real soon."

I rose to my feet and led Mara back into the condo, closing the door behind me. It was going to be a long six-month wait, but the promise of what I always dreamed of at the end of it was going to be worth it. I was finally a somebody… a somebody to someone and that someone was a somebody to me.

The End

Coming Soon

Jase and Tiff's story- Promise Me Tomorrow- Book 3 in The Witness series

Becoming Somebody Playlist

Break Free by Ariana Grande

Somewhere Out There by Our Lady Peace

Habits by Tove Lo

I Will Let You Go by Daniel Aheam

Words by Skylar Grey

Animals by Maroon 5

Take Me Home by Cash Cash

Jealous by Nick Jonas

Baby Don't Lie by Gwen Stefani

All of Me by John Legend

The Heart Wants What it Wants by Selena Gomez

Constant Craving by J2 and Lesley Roy

Other Works

by H. D'Agostino

The Second Chances Series

Unbreak Me- book 1

The Boy Next Door- book 2

The One That Got Away- book 3

Inside Out- A Second Chances Novella- book 3.5

Fallen From Grace- book 4

The Family Next Door- book 5

The Shattered Series

Destined (Shattered #0.5)

Shattered (Shattered #1)

Restored (Shattered #2)

Renewed (Shattered #3)

Fated (Shattered #4 Cam and Avery)- Coming Summer 2015

The Broken Series

Irreparably Broken (Broken #1)

Saving Us (Broken #2) – coming May 2015

The Witness Series

Being Nobody- book 1

Acknowledgements

I'm always worried that I'm going to leave someone out one of these times so if I miss anyone, I'm truly sorry.

There are so many people to thank, and as I continue on in this journey of becoming a writer, the list keeps growing. I've met so many wonderful readers, authors, and bloggers over the course of the past year that I can't even begin to name you all. Thank you from the bottom of my heart. Meeting you at signings and hearing from you on the various social media out there is just the boost my heart needs. I appreciate all of you, and I don't have the words to truly express that.

Thank you to my wonderful, supportive, awesome beta Angie for all your hard work on this book. I know I make you want to throw your kindle sometimes, but you're always honest with me, and have just the right words to keep me going. You chime in at just the right moment and seem to know exactly when I just need to vent. You aren't just a blogger in my book, you're a true friend. I can't say this enough. I had a blast in Indy and can't wait to hang with you and the Twinsie's again.

A special thank you goes out to Twinsie Talk Book Reviews. Thank you from the bottom of my heart for setting up and coordinating a kick ass blog tour. I love you guys, and I love how much you love my books.

Thank you to all the bloggers who have supported me and pimped this book out. Posting teasers, joining blog tours, and spreading the word about Sam and Dev. Sweet and Naughty Book Blog, M&D's Have You Read Book Blog, Eye Candy Bookstore, Book Boyfriend Hangover, Author Groupies, United Indie Book Blog, and so many others just to name a few.

Thank you to MJ Fields for hooking me up with an awesome new cover designer. It looks amazing. Thank you for all your help in making several new connections in the book world. I can't put into words how happy I am.

Thank you to Kelsey, you are an amazing photographer and thanks to you I now have a one of kind cover for this book.

Thank you Kari for doing an amazing job on this cover and all the swag that goes with it. You are awesome, and your speed and attention to detail is astounding.

Thank you Rebecca for your awesomeness and editing ninja skills. Yes, I think I made up a new word. I'm good at that, and you know it. LOL Your speed behind a computer amazes me, and I love reading your comments.

And finally...

Thank you to all the readers out there for loving my books and wanting to know more about The Hottie Alpha a.k.a Devlin Ford. I hope he lived up to all your wildest fantasies, and I can't wait to share Jase's story with you in Promise Me Tomorrow.

About the Author

H. D'Agostino currently resides in Syracuse, NY with her husband, two children, two dogs, and three cats. Originally from Harrisburg, NC, she attended UNC Charlotte and received a BA in Elementary Education with a concentration in Math. Heather loves hearing from her fans.

You may follow her on Facebook at www.facebook.com/H.DAgostino.Author

Or on her website H. D'Agostino- Books at http://hdagostinobooks.weebly.com

Or on Twitter at hdagostino001